A Different Road Home
Through a Silent Storm

M. T. Lange

Lange Publishing

New York

Lange Publishing

Publisher's Note: This is a work of fiction. Names, characters, places, and incidents are a product of the author's imagination. Locales and public names are sometimes used for atmospheric purposes. Any resemblance to actual people, living or dead, or to businesses, companies, events, institutions, or locales is completely coincidental.

Cover Design Judy Bullard

Editing Carol Roman

ISBN 978-1-7328496-6-2

PCIP-Publisher Cataloging in Publication

Cataloging Information

Lange, M.T.

Dedication

To those whose lives changed because of war.
Thank you for your service and sacrifice.

To Family and Home

Contents

The Fifth Season

An incubation

cocooning thoughts and experiences drawing

us into a chrysalis,

encasing the moment.

We are frantic stowaways,

masked and banded by a common enemy.

March 2020

Day 1

The old woman sat on the porch. It was mid to late morning, on an outstanding fall day. Two of the youngest grandchildren were in the yard playing their own version of cricket, soccer, or beat the ball. It didn't matter what they called it. They were content. She smiled, listening to their chatter. The sun was warm, but not too warm. It was perfect. No breeze and early enough for the heat not to be overbearing. Trees stood motionless. She loved this homestead. While the house, barn, and land were not pretentious, they nestled at the end of a road with a view of the mountains that was matchless.

Behind the house, at the top of the hill, was a pond about the size of five acres. The area was full of life. Beaver occupied the territory, mostly at one end, creating a kingdom of their own. Along the banks early in the morning and at dusk, deer appeared regularly. With the surrounding meadow, it made a world apart. What else could anyone need? The pond was spring fed and there was no shortage of fish. Though it was fall, blackberries and raspberries were in abundance, so it was not out of the question for the bears to come. Nature was rich. There was peace here, a sense of calm nourished by familiarity and a quiet reverence.

* * *

A reversed wind suctioned her breath away while her eyes, in terror, scanned an unfamiliar landscape. The room was chilly. Sounds muffled. A wildness was overtaking her. There were others speaking, but she couldn't understand. The headgear blocked what they were saying. She couldn't clearly see their faces. Everything was exaggerated, almost fantastical. Eyes were bulging. Cumbersome suits of different colors mixed with a tangle of webs surrounding her; yet didn't impede the strangers from their tasks. She felt as if she couldn't breathe. Life was slipping away. A terror gripped her throat and chest tightly, stealing every attempt at a breath.

"She's crashing. I'm going to intubate." Only a moment passed. "I'm in." There was a sound of movement. Things were clanging. Delia was aware of gowned figures moving about abruptly. They were wielding utensils with gloved hands connecting the webs that held her.

The old woman drifted, hearing the commotion, but she was in another place.

"Her pressure is dropping."

The doctor spoke up. "Vitals are weak, and so are the lung sounds. Was she tested? Anyone. C'mon, answers please."

The nurse noted the old woman had just come in. She had been sick for a few days according to family, but struggled with her breathing today. They administered a test, but there were no results yet.

"Okay, be careful, people. Let's get her comfortable."

Her breathing steadied and improved slightly.

"Where was this place? I've been here before."

She felt light. Set apart, removed, but less fearful.

Her eyes struggled to open, but couldn't conquer anything sustained.

"Hello, Delia. You should feel better soon. We had to put a tube in to help you breathe. You're getting fluids and medicine so you can relax. Rest up for a while. We'll keep checking on you. No one can come in, but your daughter brought you here, and I will update her. Try not to struggle. I know the tube takes getting used to. Staying calm is important. You should feel better soon."

The old woman was panicky. It had shown in her restlessness. Her caretakers did the best they could to bring calm. They sedated her. Briefly, before slipping into a deep sleep, clipped glimpses of her surroundings instilled more panic. They set her heart in motion, beating rapidly and irregularly. She knew she needed to relax. With that thought, she drifted again, sensing the same place as before. It encircled her calmly. She remembered hearing about experiences like this. The near-death ones, out of body, following the light, but that wasn't what this was. She wasn't in control. Her eyes were closing — no opening. She could feel a cool breeze and smell salt. It made her feel young.

* * *

The waves grabbed her toes, sending chills throughout her body. It was early summer. The water was rough and cold. It looked as if it would be sunny, but the weather forecast called for a storm later in the day. The waves were breaking farther out, then building again, a choppy sort of picture.

The ocean was mesmerizing. Even at an early age, walking along the beach at either end of the day captured her. The beach was emptier at those times, and it was much easier to focus on the natural details. The colors of the water changed. Sometimes, it was blue green, other times, a bluer gray. Before a storm, it might be a choppy brownish color. The light also changed the water. She loved it when it was smooth like glass, but that was often a sign of dangerous weather. She loved that too. But it was already beyond that point. Conditions were building for bad seas.

They (her cousins) were surely looking for her, sent out by her mother. The problem — she would stay away too long or not say where she was going. Either way, it got her in trouble, but not the way most people would think. The times were not like today. It was less dangerous. This was a beach community and a few miles from the amusement portion of the boardwalk, which was commercial, noisy, and crowded. The weather was bristling. But no one was in a hurry. People were fishing. Some would get lucky. She loved to see the ones who caught sand sharks. That's what the kids called them. They looked like small sharks, only a couple of feet long, but interesting. Then you had the couples, holding hands and whispering or laughing, secretly sharing. The runners were typical finds, as were the shell seekers. This might not be everyone, but it was a slice of the population, the regulars. She didn't know where she fit in or if she did. The ocean captured her. She was waiting for something; isn't everyone?

Her eyes fixed on the horizon, searching it out. An unshakable feeling arose—something was just out of reach. Confused for a moment, it passed as she heard her name.

"Delia, your mom wants you back at the bungalow. She's not happy when you take off telling no one." It was her cousin, Kathy. Relief arose. Kathy was one of three daughters of her mother's sister; she was a few years older. They got along well. Her aunt's girls, along with their grandmother, were part of the beach crew every year. The cousins were more like sisters and knew how to have fun. Some years, the family spent the entire summer on the shore. Those were the best times. Every one of them brought treasured memories. She was thinking when Kathy shook her and said, "Hey, Delia! Focus, will you? We're going into town today to go shopping. You're holding everything up. Delia..."

* * *

"Delia, Delia," again the shaking but the smell. It wasn't fresh or salty. It was more of the stale, lifeless smell, a cleaner of sorts, piercing and alcohol like. She was trying, but just couldn't seem to get her eyes open. It was stronger, and she felt colder. The voice wasn't her cousin, nor was it her mother. She was uneasy, but not fearful.

"Delia, how are you feeling today? Your vitals seem better this morning. Can you hear me? Maybe open those eyes? Your daughter sent in some music for you. She put a playlist together of oldies, church songs, and even classical pieces. You're quite an aficionado of the sixties, though, even a rebel of sorts, Laura Nyro and Judy Collins? Hadn't heard those in years. As soon as the doctor sees you, we'll get that music going. What do you think?"

Another nurse came into the room and asked, "Anything?" The first one replied, "She seems stronger but hasn't come to. That's what we're waiting for. It could go either way. She is positive, and this virus is insidious. We don't have a lot of answers and need to be on guard, taking nothing for granted. We've seen strange and deadly complications. You think there's a rebound and then a crisis. You can almost see her fighting."

* * *

The fierceness of the waves was growing. The sky was darker. She wanted to stay longer, but Kathy was determined to get her back so they could go to town across the causeway. Besides some shopping, and despite there were only a few stores to explore, the cousins were looking forward to eating out and catching a movie. In everyone's eyes, the storm was the perfect opportunity for that kind of day. Delia agreed, but leaving the beach when things were just getting interesting was a disappointment. Town would be a diversion and driving over the causeway watching the bay with the wind and waters stirring was a sight she expected and enjoyed.

She was feeling off. Allergies were always a problem in the summer, as well as bug bites. Reactions never failed to come at a bad time. The ocean had distracted her. Sitting out on the deck last night left her with brutal bites. Her mom would say, "It's because you're so sweet!" That offered little comfort. The mosquitos were bad at the shore and so were summer allergies. In those days, you didn't see specialists and get all kinds of tests to combat whatever. You just put up with the discomfort. So, Delia was used to it. Too bad the timing was off, especially when they had plans. Her father said to put vinegar on the mosquito bites, it would help with the itching. She was never keen on that and didn't do it. Her father put vinegar on everything, even his sunburn, which could be significant with his fair Irish complexion. He wasn't with them this week. They could stay at the shore for the summer because her parents, who both worked, took turns. One would take a vacation while the other worked. Her aunt also worked and would be in the mix of turns. Anyone working would come on the weekends, and the bungalow was busy and packed. Her grandmother was there for the duration. It was a big family and other clans of cousins came to the shore but rented separate cottages. The system the adults used made it possible to stay for extended periods. Those were the happiest times, the beach, boardwalk, drive-in movies, cookouts — what more could anyone want? She knew the movies were on tonight's agenda. Having a swollen ankle develop from the mosquito bites hurt and was annoying; that would not deter Delia, not when shopping, eating out, and a movie were concerned. She didn't feel well, though. There was an aching... she felt dizzy, but dismissed it.

Day 2

Delia Brown had 2 children. They were local, a son and a daughter. Together, they had blessed their mother with six grandchildren. They were on top of things as much as was possible during these desperate and strange times. Hospitals and medical facilities did not permit admittance to anyone other than patients during the pandemic. Pandemic—the buzz word; the focus and controller of every aspect of their lives. With its onset, most never dreamed of the extent of the changes, or the lives that would be lost. Many were stuck on conspiracy theories and plots. Karen and her brother, Tim, only knew one thing. Their mother was in the hospital, in an ICU bed, just like that. They didn't care about politics.

The siblings drove each other crazy, trying to figure how and when it could have happened. The truth, they didn't know. For them, the family was beyond that. They lived in an area that was a tourist attraction during the summer and fall months, and even during the long winters, but Delia didn't go out a lot. Church and shopping presented a few choices in a rural environment. They had attended small barbeques, but they were outside, with no sizeable crowds. Information that didn't matter now. They had to deal with today and monitor the family members.

Tim had a comfortable way with people, but Karen was more business-like, information oriented. She would be the one to talk to Dr. Levin, who was the new resident at Community Memorial Hospital. Talk, video chat. Those were the options, but she was grateful for it. Dr. Levin appeared on the screen and smiled. Karen hadn't realized her mother's doctor was a woman and so young.

"Hi, I'm Alina Levin, your mother's doctor. You know she has tested Covid positive. We have her sedated and intubated. Delia has stirred, but we can't really say she has come fully awake. Her vitals are stable; her breathing was quite labored but has steadied. We have her on fluids and antibiotics. She is stable, but very ill at this point."

"Doctor, what do you think are her chances? This has all happened so quickly. We can't even figure the exposure."

Dr. Levin replied, "That's the problem. There's a community spread, obviously. We're seeing the numbers rise. It may be slower upstate, but it's here, especially with the surge during the tourist seasons. There are asymptomatic people who also make it difficult to contain things and harder to accept the seriousness of what is happening. It's understandable that people want to be outside and social. Focus on taking care of yourself and the rest of the family for the next couple of weeks."

"Couple of weeks?"

"Yes, this doesn't seem to be a quick experience, although things continue to change. It will be important to see how far it goes and how well your mom will do. I would encourage a quarantine among your family members. Keep track of what occurs and let us know. Self-quarantine. That's important to keep the spread from occurring."

Karen continued the conversation, but there wasn't any news that could change the current situation. It was a challenge, and one for which Karen had little patience.

Later, Tim, her brother, stopped over to see how their mother was doing. All Karen could say was nothing really had changed. They considered likely points of exposure. The only thing they could come up with was the county fair that drew crowds from a few townships. That was several weeks ago.

Tim said, "The fair is a possibility. We went on Saturday with the kids, yours came too, and by the evening the crowd had doubled. You know how people look forward to that event. But mom didn't go to the fair."

Karen offered, "There was the barbeque?"

* * *

Several family groups within the larger cousin circle had left the city and moved upstate; back then, people were on the move out of the cities to less populated areas. The O'Malley family moved years ago, and Delia was always grateful her cousins had moved upstate with them. Her uncle traveled as part of his work, so her mother and aunt had conjured the plan that both families move upstate together. Each had their own homes in the same neighborhood. Everyone was content about the built in support system. Holidays, birthdays, and events were on the calendar. You always had a cheering section for anything that you did or for any help that was needed, if you wanted it or not.

Today was a picnic celebrating her and her cousin Marie's graduation from High School. She lay in bed and didn't want to get up yet. Delia looked forward to this day. Her eyes glanced above at the window framing a perfect sky. She smiled. Marie was a year older than Delia, who had skipped a grade. There was always a slight angst about Delia intruding upon Marie's school life and friends, but it wasn't serious. She was young, only seventeen, since her mother never sent her to kindergarten, which was an option back in the day.

It was a small town and a tight-knit community, even if you weren't talking about cousins. With the girls, the family had planned the graduation parties together at a local park, which had a small lake. It looked as if it was going to be a beautiful day and just made sense since the celebrations drew from the same group of people. The park provided the perfect venue for a picnic and barbeque. They had secured the spot for the parties a couple of months earlier. The decorations were simple; it would be a buffet with a boom box providing the music. Uncomplicated.

Mike was coming to the party, and that was more exciting for her than anything else. They had met on Memorial Day Weekend a couple of years ago and had been together since. A summer crush is what her father thought at the start. He raised his eyes keenly and was more protective ever since the accident, a car crash that had taken her mother. Everything changed. Everything. Her father, for sure. When you lose someone, that's how it is, of course, but he really changed. Within weeks, he was acting as if her mother hadn't been there. The goal was to keep things afloat and help Delia feel normal, but that's not how it goes. He didn't overlook his sons, but there was an ease with the boys. Delia was his girl and the youngest. Concerning interactions with his daughter, they both stumbled around. That was seven years ago. Delia knew her father loved her. She wished he would step back. That wasn't going to happen, not even today. Thomas O'Malley wasn't the type of man to step back.

Graduation from high school is a rite of passage, a long-awaited one. Today was a celebration. For a parent, her dad, it was a bittersweet day. What Delia understood, it was a day of crossing into her future. She had gotten a job as a receptionist for a small local company, and planned to take a few courses part time at the community college. It was a solid enough plan to start her into what most would consider adulthood. She had always been steady. If a word could describe her, it would be that—steady. Her father wasn't even close to hearing about adulthood or acknowledging Delia in that way. He would say, "You're my little girl and always will be." She was worried how he would feel about Mike if the relationship moved forward. One step at a time. She had gotten an older car, which was a step too. It added a sense of freedom and choice. Change was coming. It was in the air.

A smile came across her face. A clear view of the lake presented a calm picture. The road veered off to the right and followed the water to the park's entrance. Their pavilion was on the water's edge and had a canopy and rows of tables with grills at the lakeside. Her grandmother and aunt were already there, and her cousins. She was glad to see them. They weren't together as much as they used to be. The vacations by the shore had fallen off. Her two older cousins had graduated a couple of years ago and were working. The oldest cousin, Jeanne, was even engaged. That caught Delia's attention and she let herself think, *What if? What if Mike and I got engaged?* These thoughts were not so out of character for a young girl who had a boyfriend, especially in troubling times. Traditions were failing and all the rules broken, whether moral, political, or civil. The term that burned into the headlines was "the establishment." Conflicts brandished merciless confrontations with everything familiar.

There was a war across the sea, and there was a war here at home. It was seeping into every crevice of the familiar. The thought of being married was settling amidst the chaos. It motivated Delia. She wanted a family and a stable home life. Her life had been a good one so far and it wasn't selfish or about her only. She was community minded, helped where she could through church and town events. Being involved in volunteer activities was appealingly positive. This was another example of the reach for adulthood. She would be content to have a normal life. To her, that started with a husband. Mike had a job at a gas station and worked a lot of hours. His goal was to have his own mechanic's shop. Again, another solid piece to the picture. He would be here for the party, but later.

Until then, she planned to enjoy the day, be content. The weather was perfect, sunny, but with a slight breeze off the water. People were in good spirits. Some were swimming; others were at the volleyball net. Of course, any kind of party called for food, and there was no shortage of it. A crowd huddled around the multiple tables covered with food spilling onto plates packed high. Guests were busy talking and eating.

It was good, all good. She turned just as Mike was heading from the parking area to the pavilion. He got out a little early and didn't want to miss the big day. Just as Delia was about to speak, she spotted her father heading their way. He looked serious. This was it! The clash of the titans. On his face was a look that encompassed everything from uncertainty to an impending inquisition. Time to break away for a walk. A distant cousin showing up and giving her father a hug while immediately engaging him in a conversation saved them. Her father was reluctant; the couple was grateful.

Mike and Delia walked towards the water, laughing with their backs to her father. "That was great timing."

"You know it. Cousin May will keep him busy for a while." They enjoyed the moment. These days, you had to live that way. The weather, friends, family, Mike, the lake... What could be more perfect?

* * *

Something changed. The water was perfect, but it was different. It was clear, but mildly rough. That made it interesting. No one was around. She thought that was strange. There seemed to be more waves coming. They were beautiful. The number increased. Looking towards the horizon, one stood out and looked bigger. The white water was powerfully churning as the height of the wave was building. It crossed her mind that it could overtake her, but she didn't move or look back at the shore, only at the wave. As it came closer, the size was almost freakish, but it didn't frighten her. There would be no jumping this one; she would go under—dive just before it hit her. There it is. She swam down but caught the tumult of the enormous wave and felt herself rolling over and over underneath it. At one point, she was scraping the bottom. Fear rose as she gasped for breath by mistake. She couldn't stop her reaction and tried to remain calm. Another wave was coming. There was always another wave.

* * *

The alarms went off. Nurses ran in, checking the lines and vitals. Dr. Levin was next. "Delia, not this. Let's go." Her rhythm returned. They took the steps which were always taken. The AEDs, the med adjustments, finally, a sinus rhythm. "Okay, she's stabilized. That was a surprise. Delia's been doing okay. I'd like her to wake up and get off the ventilator. She isn't ready, but she's holding on." Turning to the nursing staff, she said, "I plan on being here. Took another shift. You may have to come and find me, but do it if you need anything." They nodded and spared any comments. Everyone was tired. The young doctor wondered about these incidents. What was triggering Delia's reactions? There was something about her.

She rested. Her dreams were less troubled, and her countenance showed she had settled in another world with its own ebb and flow. Sometimes, it was peaceful; at other times, there was a struggle. Now, in her own place, she was content. Leaving Delia's room, the doctor headed to a bunk to get some sleep. It was going to be a long night. Sometimes you could sleep and feel refreshed, but it had been a rough few days, more admissions and the stress of the numbers. Two of the staff were now Covid positive. That was unsettling. It was a small hospital and rural. Though the staff was great, the limited resources were problematic. Ventilators, PPE, cleaners had become priceless in the current crisis, and dominated every news broadcast or staff meeting. A different job and a move, especially to a dramatically contrasting area from what she knew, appealed to Alina Levin. But this?

Day 3

The day looked different. It was chilly. There were always transitions with the seasons. Temperatures could vary forty degrees in a day. She had opened the window, and the temperature had dropped. The airflow made sleeping more enjoyable. There was a freshness in the room that brought expectation, hope for the day. Hope was necessary when so much was in turmoil. Lately, people have been fighting or stressing about everything. It didn't matter if it was morality, school, war, drugs, politics, religion—everything. Hairstyles brought contentious comments. She was thinking of Mike and smiling about his shoulder-length blonde hair. Parades, rallies, protests were the norm. Campuses were no exception; they were epicenters for discourse. Yes, that would be a better choice of words to describe arguing in an academic setting and justifying it. The college was considering ending the semester early, with all the protests and police interactions. It was occurring around the country, and even locally. There was talk of not having regular finals. She didn't know where that was heading and didn't want to think about it. That wasn't her problem yet. Delia leaned into the turmoil, but not today; today it was fishing. She just couldn't get out of bed yet, too comfortable. Then...

The alarm went off. 5:30 AM. She had to get up. Today would be different. No classes or work. She was going to the lake, even had some gear. She had surprised Mike before and shown off her skills, having fished with her brothers and father. It wasn't high on the list of her favorite things to do, but today she and Mike were renting a small motorboat at the bait shop about halfway up the lake. The intention was to spend as much time out on the water as possible. She had packed a picnic lunch. There were small islands here and there on the lake. They would stop at one for a picnic. For the morning, there was a thermos of coffee and Danish. She knew he would be on time. She felt as if she knew everything about him. They had been together for a while, working their way through high school and now college. When summer classes started, she enrolled at the community college part-time. The campus was about 40 minutes from town. Delia made friends and settled in. Mike was going to catch the fall semester. She had hoped they would start school together, but he wanted to work more hours and save money for the future; that brought a smile.

Life was always on hold, but not in an ideal place. The Vietnam war was driving people in so many directions and hung over every 18-year-old male's head. Delia fought the thought. *Would this be the time?* No one wanted to go. What are we doing in a war halfway around the world fighting in jungles, and for what? That was the prevailing complaint, and the answer was all-encompassing — to stop the spread of communism. You didn't have to be a political activist. Like it or not, circumstances forced you to take a side. Though the draft hung over the heads of all young men, the privileged found their way out more often. Most suffered through the lottery every time a drawing came up. You registered when you were 18, by your birthdate, they calculated your number. Mike's birthday was coming up, and they had already been through this lottery once. Delia didn't want to think about it; yet, among their friends, the conversation was always there. Some were 2-S deferred; others were going to ride out whatever happened; there were those who said they just wouldn't go. If called up, they were heading to Canada, leaving everything and everyone behind. They had at least one good friend who would do this. It wasn't an idle threat. That's just the way it was. Another friend had been a paratrooper and through an intel error, the platoon dropped behind enemy lines. The enemy encircled them, and it was believed they injured or killed everyone. That was all his family knew right now. The war reached out and infected everything.

But not today. The sun, the lake, fishing, a picnic— perfect! Her brother, Finn, yelled from below, half asleep, mumbling about why he had to get up, saying Mike was there. Delia came down and around the bend in the stairwell that led to the hallway. He looked up at her. She loved his smile. A quick hug and they were out the door. Delia didn't want to waste a moment. She also didn't want any prolonged interaction with her father. She had told him what they were doing, the timeline, Mike's parents' camp for dinner, and provided their phone number. Everything. But her father was never happy with anyone she dated. She liked to think she saw a soft spot in him for Mike because he was such a hard worker. But her father didn't change easily. There was a quick, pretty ride to the lake that was becoming a habit now when the weather was good. It was cheap enough to rent the boat; the picnic lunch was not that costly either and the poles were old. A nice day was more than affordable and brought a diversion from all the troubling events.

They had lost friends in the war and through politics. Others came back from Vietnam changed and not in a good way. It was a heavy season and hard to put out of your mind. There was little relief. It seemed you were always waiting for something, for someone to deploy, or come home. You waited for a word. Unfortunately, some words you didn't want to hear.

But again, it was a beautiful day. She devoted today's thoughts to the fish, hoping for a bite. It seemed like forever, though well worth it when you spent time with someone you loved. The small lake was peaceful and a great escape. Mike's parents had a camp with access on the very north end. They would rent the little motorboat, fish, picnic, and then head towards his parents' place for dinner.

These were happy days away from the stress of school or work. The water was beautiful. She loved the lakes. This one was quiet too, as most camps surrounding it were owned by locals, so fewer tourists. The fish weren't biting. They laughed; it wasn't about the fish. It was about time, peace, nature, everything good. The talk was easy until Delia brought up the lottery. It was gnawing at her. She felt more uneasy than in the past. Mike's number was low, but he had made it before and was hoping for the best. He worked in town and didn't plan on going to college full time. That could be the problem. If you were in college full time and kept your average up, you could qualify for a 2-S student deferment. He simply wanted to keep working.

Delia hated the conversation, and it was looming, stealing the perfect day. Mike could see her face change and spoke up in a matter-of-fact way. "Let's not ruin this day. The sun is shining; the fish aren't biting, but oh well. I'm sure you packed a great lunch. Let's find a spot to set up our picnic and fish close to shore for a while; the sunnies or rock bass might be biting." He could always fix a situation with just the right words. Yes, she thought, *let's enjoy the moment.*

As with every perfect day, the wish is it wouldn't end. It was late afternoon, and that end was impending. They caught some trout and headed to Mike's parents' camp. She liked his parents. They were easy-going and comfortable. That was about the best word to describe the Parkers. The plan was to cook out. Mike had to work that evening so they would get back to shore in time for him to make his shift at the station. They pulled up to the dock. His parents were sitting outside. As they got closer, Delia sensed something wasn't right. Their faces looked serious. On the table, next to Mike's dad, was a letter. His hand was resting on it. Its appearance captured her breath. His dad and mom remained motionless. After he secured the boat, she and Mike walked over to them. His dad handed it to him. Without hesitation, he opened it in a matter-of-fact way. For a moment, he paused and then quietly said, "I've been called up."

Delia will always remember that moment. Events leading up to it had been perfect. Her graduation party, perfect. They had plans, at least for work and school. Everything seemed steady, providing a path to move forward to a future. Even some of the harder talks they had shared faded with the sun when out on the water.

"I report in ten days. Not much time to get things together."

"Ten days," said Delia in a high-pitched voice. "Ten days. What about a deferment? Can't you get a student deferment?"

"Not now. It's too late. I planned to work for a year so I could buy my car outright and get a little money together. Maybe take a couple of classes. Going part time will not cut it and I haven't even started the process."

"No! No! That's not fair. Who wants to fight this war? Why do you have to go? Why does anyone have to go? No! No! It can't be true."

"It'll be all right. I promise. I'm drafted, but that doesn't mean I'll wind up in Vietnam. Let's take one day at a time."

Mike's dad jumped in and suggested that they work on having dinner. They had prepared an enjoyable meal, and it was a beautiful day. The water was soothing and inviting, though he doubted they would do any swimming or boating. His mom was distressed but for the sake of her son and Delia, she pulled it together and followed her husband's lead, trying to bring calm and some normalcy. That news was the last thing she wanted to hear. Other mothers in their small community had sent sons and daughters overseas, and the stories were nightmares. The evening news broadcasts were showing footage from Vietnam and Cambodia. It was hard to even comprehend watching a war almost present time. As much as everyone tried, the conversation was minimal. It was a matter of going through the paces of cleaning up after dinner and somehow finishing the evening that was over before it started.

After dinner and an attempt at a reasonable visit, Mike said they needed to head back across the lake. He had to get Delia home and get to work. He hugged his parents. His father's grip lasted longer, almost to say it would be all right. But the day had gone from perfect to other worldly. Delia felt she was in a fog that was weighty and all enveloping. She couldn't see her way out and felt a growing anxiety stealing her breath.

* * *

"C'mon! You'll be okay. She's having a seizure. Let's get some Ativan—now. It seems every time we make some progress, something happens. The fever was down. We're finding more and more about the myriad symptoms and effects of this virus. The list is always changing. It's almost impossible to keep up. How has she been today? It looks as if, until now, it's been uneventful. Can you note anything that changed?" She stressed-*anything!*

A nurse replied, "Today's been the same as every other day, and then in a moment, this. She comes out of these incidents and is stronger than most of the patients her age. I hope she recovers."

As quickly as it began, Delia relaxed. The seizure subsided, but she was straining. You could see it in her face, almost as if she were saying "no", moving her head somewhat and wincing.

"Do you think she was dreaming, Doctor?"

"Probably not, though there are some who say it happens or can happen. Whatever it was, it had passed. It's about time for you to wake, Delia. Stop scaring everyone like that. You have a family waiting for you. Time to wake up."

There was no movement. She had lapsed back into her world. One that Dr. Levin hoped Delia would soon leave. They found the longer you stayed on a ventilator, the chances for recovery seemed to dwindle. There were so many who were sick. Every day, the numbers were worse; other parts of the country were increasing at an even more alarming rate. It was better in the northeast; but the lockdown pressed on people's emotions, finances, relationships regardless of location. None of that even touches on school closings and stay at home orders, and the reopening process. People were at the breaking point.

Alina Levin was in her first year of residency. It was a small hospital, and though near to a few cities, it was an extremely rural area dominated by the vastness of the Adirondack mountains. She was from the south, a military family. Her mother and father had been in the army. They were rangers and were often away for long periods. Her father's parents raised her, making life suburban and city-like. After college and all the work she had put into becoming a doctor, she felt she needed something different. Her mother had passed away a few years earlier in Afghanistan. Her father was career military and overseas. Alina knew little about the mountains, and she didn't really know anything about the northeast. The Adirondacks seemed appealing. There was a drive within, pushing her for something new. Other hospitals were closer to home, but she wanted that change. New York, downstate and upstate, were offering relocation packets and salaries that were dramatic. The appeal was great as she wanted to pay something back to her grandparents, though they weren't looking for anything in return. They loved Alina and were more like parents than grandparents.

Her parents had put a plan in place because they were away so much. She loved her grandparents and stayed local for med school. But now... surely there were enough excellent opportunities in Texas? Reluctantly, they finally understood her desire to travel. When an offer came from a northern hospital, they were sad but accepted her decision. Alina took it. No sooner did she arrive at her assignment, the pandemic broke loose. With that, double shifts and one hour running into another were the norm. Some of it was the outcome of local hospital staff leaving to help in the larger city hospitals, where staff shortages abounded. Life was not her own. Everyone was on a trajectory to places they never dreamed they'd go, to face situations they didn't want and shouldn't have to face. This was life now. Alina Levin got the change she wanted. It wasn't all bad. She was a hard worker and helpful to the other staff. That was a sure way to win friends. Alina didn't do it with winning friends in mind; she was helpful by nature. Towns canceled many typical summer events, leaving a few in place, but a social life during this strange season was almost unreachable. Along with everyone else, she was trying to find things to do. She found a small lake and park, perfect for walking her dog and sitting. Alina loved the water. It brought a calm and slowed her down.

Day 4

She was drifting. The way back to the dock was quiet. Delia calmed herself into resignation. Mike had little to say. The sun was lower in the sky, only not ready to set. It was earlier than they planned. The news cut the evening short. He stopped the boat about fifty feet offshore. Delia asked what was going on. Mike looked at her. It was a look that pierced her and frightened her at the same time.

"Let's get married now. We can hope I won't go to Vietnam. If we're married, when I get out of training, we can probably get housing wherever they send me. The one thing about the service is we may not be rich or in charge, but they'll be some benefits for you." A moment passed. "It's not like we weren't thinking about it."

When he said this, she smiled; he was right. She never expected it, but they both knew it was true and the direction was leading to marriage. That's why they had jobs and didn't want to go away to school or get into debt. Delia thought, *what about my father?*

"How can we? I'm seventeen. My father will never agree. It's a month until my birthday."

"A month, only a month, separates us from this plan. Under the circumstances, he'll agree. I can't imagine he

31

wouldn't agree, not for the grief it would cause, and for a month. We'll talk to him tomorrow."

"Tomorrow, I don't think I can. It's too fast, so fast."

Delia looked distressed. Mike had no desire to upset her. The day had turned from perfect to horrifying. Within a matter of a few hours, life changed. They were happily looking forward to a future and had all the next steps worked out. But now...

Delia was home early. Her father was up. All she wanted was to go to bed. That wasn't meant to be. He was talkative, calling her to come into the living room and asking about her evening. He almost seemed happy because she had gotten home earlier than he expected. Delia loved her father. He did his best for the family, especially after her mother died. She had 2 brothers, Finn and Jamie. Three kids for a working man weren't an easy maneuver. Though he managed, it was rough. No matter how mad he made his kids, they never doubted he loved them. It was easy to see that Delia was upset. She wasn't crying; her eyes swelled red. Normally, she was sassy and ready with an answer to any question. Anyone could see something was up.

"What's wrong, Delia.? Did something happen?" She thought for a moment, struggling to find the words.

"They drafted Mike. He leaves in ten days. Nine days." She could hardly get those words out. The time was hard to process. Then she looked at her father. She didn't even think about it.

"We're going to get married."

"Married? That's impossible. You're just kids."

With that, she snapped. "Kids? Right. We're kids, but Mike can travel halfway around the world to a jungle, to some place we've never heard of and fight people, maybe kill people or be killed himself. For what? I don't even know." By this time, she was sobbing.

Her father looked instantly broken, but forged ahead. He didn't know what to do and spoke from his heart, but it wasn't what she wanted to hear.

"You're seventeen years old. That's way too young. You'll be alone. How are you going to live?"

"I'm not too young. I'll be eighteen in less than a month, less than a month, a couple of weeks, a few days. No matter what anyone says, if I were 18, I would do it. You and mom weren't much older."

"Now wait a minute." Her father was ready to roll, but Delia would not be turned.

"We don't have a minute, not one minute to waste. We're almost down to 9 days. We'll find a way. I have a job. I can wait for school. That would give me more money to live on. I'll rent some place."

"You'll what? Why don't you try to get some rest? Things will look different tomorrow." He was holding it together, but barely.

Delia squarely looked at her father and emphatically said, "I'm not changing my mind."

"That's what you think. You're only seventeen. You need my permission. I'm not okay with this. I, I can't. It's too quick, and you're just kids."

"We're kids? That again?" She started sobbing, and it broke her father, but there was no comforting her now. She ran upstairs, passing her brother on the way. He looked at his father and gestured questioningly. Seeing the look on his father's face, he knew it wasn't the time to get answers and knew there would be no suitable answers. By then, he had heard enough. They weren't the first family to face this situation. It was happening all over. Somehow, that was little comfort.

Delia and her father were in the same house, but each on the far side of a great contentious chasm. The next day was quiet. She went to work as usual. Heading out the door, she looked back when her father said to have a good day. She thought, *a good day, yeah, right!*

Mike was looking into everything he could, from conscientious objector to medical technician. It was only a remote possibility, but maybe getting a student deferment. There weren't any options. It crossed his mind. *What if I failed the physical?* That was a long shot. He called Delia and asked her to dinner. There was a little Italian restaurant on the far side of the lake, Molinari's. The food was great and cheap and had been one of their first real dates. As corny as it sounded, they thought of it as their place.

It was about six. Delia tried to get home a few minutes early to freshen up. Her father was there, but she gave him the silent treatment. She didn't want to make him feel bad. It's not like it was his fault, but she couldn't help it. There was no sensibility anywhere anymore. Life rambled on; things you had no control over and didn't believe in framed it. The doorbell rang and her father got it. He let Mike in. Delia could see on his face and with his movements that her father was at a loss for what to say. There was no room for small talk. As Delia approached, Mike said a meek, "Good night," to her father. The ride to the restaurant was equally quiet. Neither of them felt like talking.

When they got to the parking lot, he looked at Delia. "Let's do it, get married. It won't be the best way to start, but we're in love, at least I am." She smiled, and he continued. "Then it will be us deciding everything."

She was quick to reply, "How is this possible? My birthday is a week after you deploy."

"We'll find someone to marry us. It's what we wanted, right?"

She nodded, followed by a slow, rising smile. "Of course it is. I just didn't expect it right now. My father will never agree. He already said so."

Mike's answer was simple. "We'll find a way."

When they got back to Delia's house, her father was up. She dreaded it. Mike wanted to come in and talk, but she just wasn't up to it. He kissed her quickly and said that he would call tomorrow. When Delia walked in, she was about to head up the stairs. Her father called for her; she stopped on the step and looked down, her shoulders slumping. Her father stood by his chair. "Delia, please."

She softened, "Okay."

"I know this is a terrible time for you. I know I don't always have the right words, but you need to consider what's best; what's not is some hurried decision."

In a calm voice, she said, "There are no other options for us. We want to do this—now, before it's too late. There are ways.

But it all seems too complicated for the time left. We're going to try, though. I will declare emancipation, or another possibility leaves it with the judge as in the best interest of the minor. We will try. I'm just short a few days away from legally being able, and it shouldn't even be an issue."

Her father straightened and looked at her, his daughter. He could see that determination. He knew she would make it happen. Mike was a solid kid, and he knew that too. Against his better judgment, he was caving.

There was a decision to make. He could alienate Delia, who somehow would find a way. If he stopped it, he could cause a serious rift, unbridgeable, or he could let them get married. Delia could stay at home while Mike was away. He'd have his daughter and a son. "I don't know another parent who would do this." Quietly he said, "I'll sign the consent. But he better be respectful of you, take care of you..." Delia threw her arms around his neck and sobbed for a long time.

Day 5

Alina Levin enjoyed going to the park with her dog, Jax. She would laugh and call him a mutt of many colors. He was medium-sized and overly friendly. She was reserved, not introvert-like, simply the quiet type, but open when the conversation beckoned. Going to the park in late afternoon or early evening was a great release from the day's stress. Even when the parking lot looked crowded, it never felt that way. People were in their own world enjoying the water and the outdoors. This included some trails that provided needed relaxation and room for exploration. She felt the day fall off her shoulders as soon as she got out of the car. The air, the view, and the peace were nothing less than restorative.

Coming to upstate New York was a dramatic change from the hot Texas climate and lifestyle. Topping off those differences, she was anticipating snow. When she mentioned she was looking forward to winter, the hospital staff rolled their eyes and walked in other directions. Most wondered why in the world she would even consider leaving the warmer climate. Alina didn't really have any winter activities that motivated her, but she was game to try anything.

It was impossible to overlook the added curiosity of trying a completely different lifestyle. Her father's family was from Texas. Her parents met when her mom transferred there while she was in the service. It was a quick romance, with orders hovering over their heads. They loved each other and Alina. The times they had were happy. Her grandparents played a major role in her life. With her parents' deployments and changing circumstances, her grandparents were more like parents. Her mother died serving in Afghanistan. Her father came home for the funeral. There was no joy or peace when he did. Everything returned to business as usual. It was a leave; he was present but not really. Even as a child, Alina understood the pain and was grateful for her grandparents, who brought some normalcy and happiness into her life. Make no mistake, she always said that her father was supportive of her going to med school and covered most of her expenses. For that, she would be forever grateful.

Here and there, her mother had given some information when Alina questioned. The rift and silence in her mother's family grew out of their disapproval of her enlistment. Her mother had tried to sell it on every level. She would go to school, and they would pay. Her mother became a nurse; she was an officer and volunteered to go to Afghanistan, which made matters worse. That was all she knew. The military offered her the chance to explore opportunities and get an education. Time passes when people let things go. Then they almost forget; they do forget. Silence and distance become habits.

A whirring sound caught Alina's attention; almost simultaneously, a frisbee hit her head. Remarkably, Jax caught it. She turned, laughing, and running her way was Gabe Stewart, another doctor from the hospital. Gabe was out with his dog, a golden retriever who was obsessed with frisbees. The two dogs took off, not far, but obviously unconcerned with their people.

Gabe affably stated, "Hey, Alina. Didn't know the park was your stomping grounds."

"Didn't know I had a designated stomping ground."

"Just talk. Do you come here often?"

"It's a nice place to relax after work. Been wild! Don't you think?"

"I know. Almost too much to deal with. For me, getting outside helps. We live in a beautiful area. It may not have the same outlets that cities do, but cities can't enjoy their amenities now, anyway. Mostly, I'm an outside guy. The trails are great; the water is inviting. Brings a calm."

"Agreed, hey the dogs are getting pretty far from us," Alina pointed ahead.

"No worries. Got time for a hike up the trail? The one straight ahead is short and follows the lake and will come back to the parking area. Eddie and I take this one when we don't want to work too hard."

"Eddie?"

"My dog. She's an outdoor type."

"She?"

He nodded, and Alina didn't hesitate. "Sounds good. I need to head back to the hospital after. Doing a flex-kind of double." He was already moving up the trail. She smiled and took off after him.

Evenings at the hospital were quieter than daytime hours. As busy as things were, the hospital did not permit visitors. At night, it could almost be peaceful once nurses dispensed meds. Delia's status plateaued. Her family (children), Karen and Tim, were diligent about checking in for updates. They had regular telemed appointments. There just wasn't the change anyone hoped for. The hospital saw this with too many patients. The ones on the ventilators leveled out until something happened. They found it could be weeks. Then, there were those who, in a matter of a few days, had a crisis. Everything about this virus was confounding. You had symptoms; then there were new symptoms; the aftereffects of the virus kept developing. Some patients had cardiac problems. Others had chronic fatigue. But now, Delia appeared to be sleeping in her own world, on her own time.

The next day, her father held true to his word. He signed the consent. The couple was married in a small ceremony and, along with their two families, had a dinner out. By the time they got the marriage license, blood tests, and planned for the ceremony and dinner reservations, four more days had passed. The parents paid for them to rent a little cabin on Saranac for a couple of days. In less than a week, it was unimaginable how much had happened.

Delia tried holding it together. She and Mike were as happy as they could have hoped to be under the circumstances. They had been through so much in a matter of days. Time couldn't have escaped any faster. The immediate family accompanied Mike to the induction center. It was a quick ride. Other families were gathering. As the young men arrived, they were putting their belongings on the bus. They would depart soon for the base, where they would train and get orders. The entire group, draftees and families, had a sense of resignation for what those orders would be. Mike tried to stay positive, but it was a monumental task amid the current atmosphere and a sorry sight, with a sea of tears being shed on every side. They gave a five-minute warning. That made it even worse. Parents stepped back and gave the couple some room. Delia was fighting an all-out flood of emotion. One last goodbye. Mike could see her distress and said, "I love you. We can do this. It will work out. I promise." With that, she watched him board the bus. All the others were waving their goodbyes. The scene froze in time. Delia's father stepped forward and put his arms on her shoulders. She ever so slightly turned. They walked back to the car. Her father tried to get a conversation going and keep things light. It wasn't working. Delia felt drained and wanted to remember his face, his smile. Maybe that would help.

The Parkers dropped Delia and her father at home. They said goodbye and promised to keep in touch. She was grateful for them. Everyone had tried putting aside their own sense of what they felt was right to help the young couple maneuver all the events of the last days. Her father knew she wanted to be alone and rest, if that was even possible. Delia headed upstairs, saying a quick thanks and goodnight.

She shut the door to her room, leaned against it, and looked around. This had been her room for years. Tonight was unlike any other night. For the longest time, she wanted to be married to Mike and hoped her father would approve. The wedding was simple but perfect, and they even got to go to the lake, which was also perfect. What was never part of the dream was Mike being drafted. Delia knew he was hoping for another assignment, but they widely accepted most would wind up in Vietnam. She kept telling herself, don't think ahead. For today, he was safe, and so was she. Delia felt like being alone but was relieved that she was alone in her own home with family nearby.

Since she was living at home, she could afford to take classes. Originally, that was to be as full a load as possible, but she needed her job at the office, which led to curbing the school schedule. The busyness of the day helped time pass, providing distractions and some money. The shock of the wedding week and Mike's departure faded as she fell into a routine. She couldn't really describe the feeling as peaceful, but was quietly resigned to her new life. It was strange when she would see her friends on campus, even her cousin. There was a divide that left the high school girls turned coeds behind; however, Delia didn't fit with the adults she knew either. Her life before ended and now she was striving to find her place. If Mike had been here, it would have been easy, but as it was, this was unfamiliar territory. There were a few other young wives, but clearly, Delia was the youngest. They had attended a meeting before Mike left and received information about a wives' support group. These were cropping up everywhere, even for those who were not on a base. Delia didn't want to talk to anyone. That was just how she felt and though there were others from town who sent a family member off, there were only a couple of wives, and again, she was by far the youngest.

The new recruits were told they could write home, but that only happened twice. A phone call was possible, yet limited in occurrence. There would be a graduation of sorts. Eight weeks was an eternity. Until it wasn't. There were letters and only one actual phone call during training. Mike stayed positive, but they both felt worse after any connection. He found he was heading out for more training, AIT, Advanced Infantry Training. That sounded impressive at first, but it came to mean you were on the fast track for Vietnam. In Mike's case, so it was. They had gotten to see each other at graduation and have a day, one day. She thought he looked different when she met him after the ceremony. He was! All his hair—gone! That was the most obvious. But underneath the easy-going personality, there was a change. He was more serious, not tense, not angry, but serious. In less than two months, they had scaled the heights of emotion; then, for however trite it sounded, sunk into despair. The time came, and the day was over. She was so uneasy and on the brink of falling apart, but held it together for as long as she could. His parents were upset as well. The ride home was silent. No words or comfort could pull Delia back to solid ground.

* * *

Alina was grateful for a quiet night. It was also a Monday. Fewer tourists on weekday evenings. The numbers at the hospital were not dramatically different. Hospital procedures and life changed. The hospital canceled or postponed normal appointments. Doctors performed no elective procedures. A frightening thing was that people just weren't coming into the ER. She knew, as did all medical personnel, heart attacks, strokes, high blood pressure and other types of illnesses didn't disappear. They were out there, but people didn't want to come to the hospital; even local doctors' offices were maneuvering the same issues. Despite that, those who made their way to the hospital were very sick. Though it wasn't a massive, dense, urban area, there were significant numbers of Covid cases. Tourists, farm workers and just the fact it was summer certainly influenced the community atmosphere.

"Penny for your thoughts!" Gabe Stewart came up to the station and broke the moment.

"They probably aren't even worth a penny!" Alina smiled.

"I don't believe it! Things can't be that bad. It's just a sunny day at the lake, carefree and relaxing!"

Gabe's smile was refreshing and easy-going. He was a good doctor. Staying cool in a crisis and creative thinking were his trademarks. Everyone liked him, and if there was a critical situation, you'd want Gabe there.

Alina said, "I didn't expect to see you this shift. I was thinking about how everything has changed so much. I also have a few patients that aren't improving. It's been a slow process. You know as well as I, the longer this goes on, the less likely they are going to make it." Her face looked distressed.

"You're speaking about Delia Brown?"

"Yes, no. Okay, maybe. There's something about her. I don't know what."

A nurse approached the desk and said, "Dr. Levin, Delia Brown looks like she's coming to."

"Wow! Let's go, finally encouragement. She must have heard us talking."

They walked down the hall and took a sharp left through the door and saw the small woman; her eyes opened, looking from side to side. She was struggling to focus.

"Delia, Delia."

Her head turned ever so slightly. That was good. She had an awareness. Dr. Levin stepped in a little closer, smiling. She touched Delia's hand and introduced herself. The old woman's eyes changed. Alina could see that there was a connection. She squeezed the young doctor's hand. The tube was in place, and Delia was struggling. It could be a problem, but there was something else; something was troubling her. Her face looked so sad. The doctor leaned in. In the next moment, she lapsed back into her world. "I guess this was too much for her. Patients drift in and out." But this time was different. There was an alertness, a recognition.

"I didn't think it was anxiety."

Quietly, and under her breath, she said, "It seemed like something more. Her vitals are stable." She hoped that this was it, the breakthrough for Delia, but unfortunately, it wouldn't be just yet.

* * *

Exhaustion surrounded Delia. It was a marathon day, the drive, graduation, goodbyes. She couldn't remember ever feeling so tired. A light was on, as always, when any family was out and expected to be late. Gratefully, her brothers weren't up as she struggled to get to her room. She simply left her father standing in the hallway. Talking was something she couldn't handle now. Truthfully, she didn't feel as if she could handle anything. As she dozed off, the fleeting thought was, *it's only the beginning.*

Patterns usually change, but this one didn't. The alarm rang and disrupted a deep sleep. It was 6:30. She dreaded today. Her job, mostly, was a blessing and pleasant. The office setting and people were fine. They weren't the problem. She was so tired. Though her frame was small, she felt she couldn't lift it from the bed. Over the last two months, with the wedding, the induction and then yesterday, she had taken multiple days off. There was no way that she could call in and take another day. Maybe with a shower and coffee, she thought that her energy would improve, but it didn't. As she got up, she was suddenly dizzy and would have hit the floor, except she was close to her bed, and now frightened. That had never happened before. The room was moving. It was unsettling, but she was secure knowing that she was emotionally and physically spent, and not just from yesterday. That was the answer. It was reasonable to feel the way she did. Closing her eyes wasn't helpful, so she opened them. It passed. After dressing, Delia headed downstairs, not really looking for any kind of conversation. She thought, *That's not fair. We're family.* Everything took effort she didn't have.

Her father was at the table; so were her brothers. They were quiet. Simple nods of the head or a pass of the coffee pot or toast. Finally, her brother, Finn, spoke.

"How was your day yesterday? The graduation?"

Trying to sound positive, Delia said, "Mike looked different, almost no hair." Some quick smiles and laughs broke the tension. They asked what was next, and she explained AIT. They were more serious about that answer, knowing what it might lead to. She explained it wasn't as long as basic training and it was more focused. Then the chit chat. They had a late lunch with his parents and somewhat of a visit, but it was a long trip home and they had to start back after a couple of hours. She was tired. That was the bridge to getting up later than planned and needing to go to work.

As she got ready to walk out the door, she felt a hand on her shoulder. Turning, her father was there and drew her in. Just a hug, nothing more. It was brief and he let go quickly, turning towards the kitchen. If she let herself, she could have cried, but that didn't happen.

Work didn't make the day easier, at least not this day. Everyone was glad, congratulating Delia (and Mike) on his graduation. They had a cake. She smiled, knowing they always had cake for any remote reason to celebrate. They were kind, and it was a peaceful office. The goal was to get through today. There was something about a routine that helped when you were going through a hard time. If you had things (or a job) that had to be done, it forced you to compartmentalize problems. That's the point she wanted to get to, the routine.

A few weeks passed, and there had been 2 letters from Mike. The tone was always cheerful. He mostly had questions about home and said he had made a few friends. One was a young man who was also from upstate New York. Delia looked forward to the mail. It was a connection, even if it held little information. Then, the phone call. At first, she was excited.

They hadn't spoken since his graduation. He sounded distant; it wasn't the connection.

"It's so good to hear your voice. How are you doing?" She was overwhelmed but eked out a simple, "Okay." Her feelings were mixed, glad to hear his voice, but with a heaviness that something was coming, something she didn't want to hear.

"Well, I guess I've done such a great job that they've sent me out right away. Our platoon is top-notch, or at least that's what we've been told." She didn't remember much after that because she had fainted. Her father heard her fall and ran to the hallway. You could hear Mike on the phone calling out to her while Delia's horrified father tried to revive her. One of her brothers came down the stairs and picked her up and carried her into the living room. Her father grabbed the phone and told Mike that she had fainted. O'Malley asked what he said to her. He told his father-in-law the news, and it brought an instant understanding. The response was that he should call later, that Delia hadn't come to. Mike hurriedly stated that he was shipping out later in the evening and didn't know when he could call again. There was a frantic moment, and he said he had to go; others were waiting in line to use the phone. Then the phone hit the receiver. Delia's father went into the living room. Her brother was sitting by her side. She was stirring, but clearly not fully recovered. O'Malley told his son to call the doctor.

She didn't remember fainting, but remembered the phone call.

"Mike..."

"He had to go, Delia. There was a line for the phone. He said he loved you and would write as soon as he was able."

"No! No! No! I need to talk to him. There must be a way."

She was growing increasingly upset. Within an hour, the doctor arrived. The fatigue was weighty upon her, and she just thought maybe she could get something for it.

"Delia, you need to calm down. Getting this upset isn't good for you or the baby."

It was like everything stopped. Her father, brother, and even she felt stunned.

"The baby?"

"You didn't know?" The doctor could see the looks on their faces. It wasn't even a thought with everything else that was going on.

"You didn't suspect?" She didn't answer and was simply staring straight ahead. Her father rallied to speak.

"It's okay, Delia. Everything will be okay. I'm glad you're here. We can work this out."

The doctor was the next to step in and said that she needed to eat and get regular rest. He would give her a script for prenatal vitamins. She should come into the office soon so he could check her out completely and do more bloodwork. Delia nodded. She went to stand up but lost her balance. With the news she had received about Mike shipping out, it was as if she had lapsed into shock. Everything had grown foggy. All of it was enough, but now she was pregnant... and Mike didn't know. He had to hang up. He was shipping out, and he didn't even know the most important thing she could have told him. *A baby... what was going to happen? Her job? Doctor bills? Other than babysitting for a few of her younger cousins, she knew nothing about infants or being pregnant. What now? A wives' support group? Maybe they could be a help? Some of them were young mothers.* Her mind was racing. The doctor left, and her father encouraged her to go up to bed. He said he would bring her something light to eat. She didn't want to, but her father insisted, noting he really didn't want to see her faint and fall. Reluctantly, she got up and was lightheaded, so her father waved to her brother to see her upstairs. Events were changing more than she could have imagined.

After eating a little, she felt better and fell asleep. It was a restless sleep. How could it not have been? She woke early, before the alarm, remembering the events of the previous night. With that came a heaviness. It was almost too much, facing this day, the one she dreaded from the first. When she swung her legs over the side, she felt queasy again. *How am I going to get to work today?* There was a knock at the door, and she quietly said to come in. It was her father. A weak smile came over her face. He was bringing more food and joked, "Don't think I'm going to be doing this every day, but last night was rough, so I cooked up some eggs and bacon." He didn't demand any conversation and left the food on her end table.

It took every ounce of energy, but she got up, ate, and made it to work, which was an outlet. People were friendly, but not intrusive. Right now, that was welcome. Delia's number one goal was simple: not to think about anything. It was all too much. Get through the day. A goal that should have been simple enough. Should have been.

* * *

A double! Alina was on from the previous evening. Night shift can go either way, a real sleeper or Mach speed. Last night had been the latter. There were the typical accidents, food poisoning, and a couple of people and a baby who tested positive for the virus, as did her mother. She was only a few weeks old and was running a high temperature. Alina was concerned about whether the baby was coming close to needing a ventilator. This was a small hospital and didn't have a NICU. They were giving her fluids, antibiotics and, for the moment, keeping her with her mother. Getting things under control would be the best remedy. Enabling them to stay together and closer to home would reduce the stress of an already intense situation. The window for a decision was narrow. Alina didn't feel she could go home, and it was a moot point. She was on an already extended shift. Checking in on Delia again, while she had time, seemed to make sense. Today, they were crossing over into almost a week on the vent.

Day 6

The nurses were catching up as the shift had changed. Alina was grateful for this team. They were skilled, pleasant, and dedicated. She was content with the choice of her residency. This was a rural community hospital specifically focusing on emergency medicine. It was a mostly underserved area as far as health needs. The hospital didn't stand out for any special studies or scientists, but they had what mattered: good people. Those who knew what they were doing and put their patients before their egos. Alina had seen enough of that in larger, more urban settings. She was early in her career but knew how the self-importance a doctor or anyone showed could sour a work atmosphere. Big egos were tiring. In those cases, the patient always paid the price. It wasn't like that here. She walked into the room.

"How's Delia today?"

"No changes, doctor. She seems so close to coming around. Then nothing."

"We know people can go quite a while this way. Unfortunately, this is a new virus or variation on a virus. Patients older than Delia have come out of it after an unbelievable number of days; others don't, so we wait." She paused for a moment. "Hey, what's that playing Judy Collins? *Send in the Clowns?*"

"Yeah, her daughter put a CD together with a bunch of songs from the 60s and 70s. She said Delia would listen to them at home. We thought maybe the music might be helpful, jumpstart her, somehow, since the family can't be here to read or talk to her."

"Not a bad idea. It certainly can't hurt, especially if it is something familiar. I have always liked music from that time. My mother was a fan. Well, at least there have been no other events, no fever, seizures, or extreme restlessness. We simply wait and hope."

That was the one thing Alina hated, waiting. There were times with patients when you knew they would not make it. Sometimes, things resolved quickly and positively. Everyone was ecstatic. But there were also times like this when you did not know and had to wait. Every passing day felt like something failed, even you failed. That's where they were with Delia. She stared at the small woman in front of her, thinking, *Delia, c'mon. Wake up.*

That day when Delia had opened her eyes. There was something Alina couldn't figure. It wasn't fear or anger, but something. A question, like a light going on, a passing moment, and she drifted off. The young doctor told the nurse, who had just come on, it would be a long night. Some new admits, one an infant who tested Covid positive and was in the ICU. She was heading there now, saying how fragile the situation was. The child needed to be stronger before being transported anywhere. The mother also was positive, so there were a few moving parts in deciding what would be best at this point.

She stepped out of the elevator and heard the code. The baby... hurrying down the hallway, she entered the room. The team had moved the distraught mother to an adjoining space next to the baby. They drew the curtain, and a nurse stayed with the woman, who was crying and questioning what was happening.

Alina asked, "What are we looking at?"

The nurse responded that the baby had been struggling but took a turn for the worse and was unresponsive. Continuing to move ahead, the young doctor quickly and confidently was successful at inserting the tube. Immediately, the infant improved. Her breathing eased, and the color returned. For the moment, a crisis had passed, but this was an extremely sick child and now a child on a ventilator.

Alina calmly and quietly warned everyone how fragile the situation was. There was an uncertainty deciding to transport the pair to the larger hospital with the NICU. That probably wouldn't happen until there could be confidence in the child's stability. Understandably, the mother was upset, and she was also quite sick, but lucid enough to know how delicate everything was. Alina introduced herself and tried to calm her down as much as possible. The masks, gowns, gloves, and all the added elements of the room were not comforting. As kindly as she could, the doctor explained they had to intubate the baby, but explained she was resting now, and her breathing stabilized. For as unnerving as it was, this was the best outcome. The young mother calmed herself at least a little.

Alina's standout attribute was her compassion. A reasonable quiet was restored on the ward. She pulled up a chair and had her hand on her patient's arm. She said little, but sat. That slight touch with another caring person was as important as any medicine. On a double shift like this, in some ways, it was the best place to rest, and she knew it would help. The silence returned; the mother was resting, and the baby was peaceful. It might not last long, but whatever quiet they could gain was a win.

* * *

Delia opened her eyes. She took a minute to focus and searched for a face. There. Mr. Wells? Work? Oh No! She was shaky and questioning. She tried to sit up, but her head hurt and looking around, she was on the sidewalk. *What's going on? How did I get here?* Another face, Ella, the secretary from work. She said, "Ella, what's going...," her voice trailed off. Holding her hand, Ella tried to comfort the distressed young woman and keep her from moving too fast.

"You fainted, honey. Your head has a minor bruise. You're going to be fine; stay put till we get some help."

Help? What help? She may have thought she said those words, but she didn't. It was easy to see the confusion, and there was that bruise. Onlookers had continued to gather. She didn't say anything else, and just sat in an awkward position on the pavement. The first responders arrived from the local fire department. That only added to the stress of what Delia perceived as an already humbling situation. She tried to persuade everyone she was fine, but she had fallen, bruised her head, and was obviously confused. The EMTs told her that her blood sugar was low, which could have caused her to faint. They asked when she ate last. Delia didn't even want to respond as the last 24 hours were horrible, and she didn't really eat more than a few bites.

"Delia, Delia, you all right? What happened? What's going on?" It was her brother, Jamie. She loved him dearly, but not right at this moment. The EMTs filled him in.

"Fainted, hit her head? Again? Is the baby okay?"

That was too much information. She held her head in her hands and heard the round of comments.

Fainted? Again? What baby? These comments did not escape the people from her office and confirmed what the responders believed from the beginning: a trip to the hospital ER was a must. She wanted to fight, but was so tired and overwhelmed, she just let go and agreed. The ambulance arrived. They put her on a stretcher, which she felt was over the top, and off they went. Jamie was shouting he would be right behind them and meet her in the ER and would call dad. That was the final straw. Though she was quiet, she turned her head away from the attendant and tears streamed down her face.

It only took a few minutes to get to the ER. The attendants opened the doors of the ambulance and instantly Delia heard the familiar voice of her father, Tom O'Malley.

"Delia, honey, are you okay? You hit your head; they think you're all right. Say something."

"Mr. O'Malley, your daughter is going to be fine. She's shaken and needs to be checked out, especially if she's pregnant."

It was almost too much, never mind almost.

"Pop, it's okay. I'm fine." The entourage kept moving down the hallway and stopped at a curtained room where the nurses took over. Her father headed to a nearby waiting area, and Jamie came running in next.

"What the heck happened?" asked Tom O'Malley.

"They say she fainted and hit her head. That's all I know. I mentioned the baby, and they were concerned and checking for a concussion because she hit her head hard when she fell."

"That's great, just great. If it wasn't for bad luck..."

"I know, Pop. I'm sure she's going to be okay."

"Nothing's okay," was Tom O'Malley's annoyed response. They came to the end of the corridor and could see through a slightly drawn back curtain. Delia was sitting up in bed. A nurse was busy checking the machines and tubing. She read the disturbed looks and a quick, "I'm fine," arose immediately.

"Sure, that's why we're here," replied her father. He was a mix of sarcasm and concern. The nurse relayed that the doctor ran some bloodwork just to be sure nothing else was going on, but other than a bump on her head, she looked to be okay. Delia perked up and said she could go home when they had the test results. Her father softened, seeing that his sharpness was only making things worse. He wasn't angry with her. They were all reeling from the circumstances of the last three months. It seemed if things could go wrong, they did. With that, the doctor came in and assured them she really was all right. He added she was slightly anemic and besides the prenatal vitamins, he wanted Delia to take some iron. Other than that, she should feel better if she's eating properly. He understood the stress. Think of the baby. The trio headed home.

Delia was silent for most of the brief trip. It was across town, but didn't take very long. They turned down their street, and she took a deep breath. Her brother, who for most of their lives had been a pain, was now like her super watch dog. He jumped out of the car and ran to open her door and reach to help her out.

"I'm fine, really. I can walk by myself."

"Says the girl who fainted twice."

"I just need to eat more and get some sleep, and I'll be perfect. I don't know what I'm going to do about work." Her response was sarcastic and showed her frustration.

Her brother stepped up and said, "Mr. Wells already said to stay home tomorrow and then you could talk about it with him."

"They have been great. I just can't keep missing work."

Jamie responded. "Look for a couple of days, rest. What's wrong with that?"

She had no answer and knew he was right. Her aunt heard about the events of the day, as did half the town. That's how it is in small villages and towns. It was also their appeal.

Aunt Janie brought chicken soup, bread, cookies, and fruit. Enough for the whole family. She also brought kind words.

Dinner was more than casual. Everyone took part in the comfort food Janie had brought. For a passing moment, it was peaceful, an extraction from the day's trauma. The sofa was insulation against the bumps and bruises, but also from the humiliation of sitting on the sidewalk for what seemed an eternity, which led to the commotion of the ER. She drifted in comfort, a response to the power of the old sofa's worn state.

The others saw she was asleep and agreed that leaving her was the best action to take. It would probably be the first solid night's sleep in a while. They whispered their goodnights. Aunt Janie left. The house was quiet. Morning came and, unbelievably, Delia was asleep. Her father moved towards her and even checked if she was breathing, just as he used to when she was a baby. All was well, and he smiled, heading to the kitchen.

The aroma pervaded the house. Delia stirred. Pancakes and coffee! When she opened her eyes, it took a minute to assess what had happened. She wasn't in her room, and was dressed. Closing her eyes again seemed to be the best response. Admittedly, she felt better, more rested, but slowly, yesterday's drama came back. She was unsettled, but not as tired and not faint. Those were improvements. The pancakes and coffee were calling, and so was her father.

"Breakfast, come and get it!"

This time, Delia got up. She stood for a moment to catch her balance and focus. When she turned towards the kitchen, her brothers were making their way down the stairs. Shoving each other and fooling around, as always. It didn't matter that they were adults. They were the same, always fooling around. Both were moving faster than Delia to the kitchen. She was grateful, grateful for the things that were the same. Family. She was grateful for her father. He could be rough, but he was the most dependable person. You could count on him. For all the problems, Delia knew she had help, a loving family, and a support system.

The pancakes and coffee smelled so good, but upon lifting a fork and taking a first bite, a wave of nausea struck her; she made a mad rush to the bathroom. The men in the kitchen froze. When she came out, she felt better, but was not so sure about eating.

Conversation was light. Everyone tiptoed around yesterday's events and focused on today's schedule. Delia remembered she wasn't going to work and needed to see the doctor for further tests and prenatal vitamins. Mike. He has to know. He's going to be a father! How could she get this information to him? Somehow, she had to figure that out. Without knowing the exact locations and timing of his travel, writing was a last resort. She would do that today. Another disappointment! One of the most important events in a couple's marriage and they wouldn't be together. At least getting a letter in motion would be a step.

Her father and brothers headed out. They repeatedly kept telling her the same things, "Take it easy today! Be sure to eat. Don't exert yourself. Call if you need anything." These would become their mantra. She raised her eyebrows and a quick smile followed. Since she was off today, it made sense to see the doctor. As understanding as everyone had been, she had to have a plan for work. So, this was one thing off her list.

Dr. Stone's office was in town. He had his own clinic, apart from any hospital duties. They had a cancellation this morning. She took advantage of it. Fortunately, Delia hadn't had to visit the doctor much; she had only been to the clinic a few times. It was small but well equipped for the town and surrounding area. Having a hospital so close was also a plus. With the recent news, it was amazing to Delia how her perspective on most things was changing. She was going to be a mother. Other than the nausea, she didn't feel different, at least not in what she perceived to be maternal. As with any medical appointment, there was a wait time even in the exam room.

After about fifteen minutes, Dr. Stone gently knocked on the door and entered. He was a friendly, easygoing sort and part of the community for a long time. It was going to be a family practice in more than one way, as his own son was soon to graduate from medical school. Generations of families often built small communities and brought a sense of stability. With a friendly smile, he greeted her.

"Delia, you look much better today. I take it you got some rest."

"I did. My family is on a mission to keep me in a bubble for the next few months."

The doctor laughed and went on with the examination.

"Everything's fine, on track. We'll watch your blood pressure; but after having a good night's rest and eating, you can see they were the key to returning to normal today. You can do what you always do. Just remember to get your rest and not overdo it. I have vitamins for you. The nurse will give them to you and set up your next appointment. You'll be coming once a month for the next few months; as your time draws closer, I will see you more often."

Overall, it was an uneventful visit. Her father and brothers would be relieved with the report. It was midday by the time she got home and time to plan dinner. Staying busy and not thinking about anything was helpful. That was the new strategy. She would write the letter to Mike tonight. Everything kept changing. Time distorted. Nothing was remotely the way they had thought it would be. A simple plan at the start: graduate, save money, college part time and then get married. How could that have turned to this?

She thought, *Overwhelming! I have to stop thinking that....* Delia was sick of it. All of it. *What about Mike? He doesn't even know half of it.* Right now, it was dinner. She would focus on that baked ziti, some salad and bread. Maybe if there was energy left, some brownies. If all else failed, there was ice cream. The men of the house had a weakness for Rocky Road. The freezer always had ice cream.

Each came home insisting on an individual report. Delia knew that would be the case. It added a touch of humor which everyone needed. Dinner was pleasant, almost normal. Finn and Jamie came home first. Unknown to them, they got the shorter version. She wasn't as lucky with her father. He wanted every detail: vitamins, appointments, limitations, due date? Due date? Delia hadn't even thought about it. She knew it would be late winter to early spring, but never even pressed the doctor about when. How unlike a new, first-time mom! She didn't even think about asking. She just wanted the appointment over. Having so many involved with the news of a baby was unsettling. Tonight, though, she was grateful. It was quiet.

No one was going to allow her to do the dishes. That was fine. She had spent her whole life trying to get her brothers to do them. Now they were insisting; it was laughable. The letter. That was the next task. Delia took a shower and worked on the letter. It was work. She knew how much Mike loved her and he wanted to get married. Delia also knew that he would feel horrible not being here to see her through this unexpected event.

Day 7

The hospital was stirring. Shift changes, rounds, the kitchen, housekeeping; every corner moved with purpose. Alina would head out soon, but wanted to check on the mother and baby. She would stop in and see Delia, too. The mother was anxious, understandably, but the baby had been doing well and rested peacefully. She was stable, and it looked as if a medivac would transport her to a hospital with the appropriate NICU services. One problem solved. Alina did not know what would follow.

She almost made it to the parking lot. Not quite through the double doors, she heard a voice calling, "Dr. Levin, Dr. Levin! Wait, please." It was Cami Johnson, a nurse, an exceptional nurse, and one of the strongest links on the staff.

"So glad I caught you. We need you!"

Alina turned. "Need me? I'm already late leaving the shift, and it was a double."

"I know. Dr. Stewart called in and said he was sick, fever, chills, all the typical stuff we've been seeing. Who knows how long he'll be out once he tests? He took an at home one and will get back to us."

Alina saw the desperation. But another twelve hours?

"What about Dr. Stone? Dr. Keeler?"

"Dr. Stone's clinic called, and it's backed up with patients. He called earlier to give us a heads up; he might not make it in. I guess we're seeing the effects of a surge. Dr. Keeler left just before you. He had finished his shift and had originally come in half a day early. Dr. Stone was to be your replacement, and we were hoping for Anne Ward, the nurse practitioner, to come in. But she's going to be late because her clinic is also full. What do we do now?"

That was a good question. It was a small community hospital serving multiple towns and villages. Alina couldn't help thinking, *I guess this is what they meant on the news when talking about a summer surge.* It didn't matter that it was almost fall. That was all over every broadcast. People were being less careful. Fed up with restrictions, fear, and the constant politicizing of everything. They just wanted their freedom back and there was plenty of time left for enjoying the outdoors despite the date on the calendar. Sunshine and warmer temperatures were the carrots leading them on. Cami's voice interrupted her thoughts.

"Dr. Levin, please advise. We need some help here."

Alina turned with a weak smile and said, "I know."

She headed back to the ER. Cami wasn't far behind apologizing, understanding the weight she had dropped on Alina's shoulders.

"I'll be back out in five. Just need to collect my thoughts and change. You'll be the charge nurse. I guess you already knew that. Call over to Harrison's Landing and see when that NP, Anne Ward, can come. I know it's a long shot. If we catch any kind of break, we'll have a meeting at the nurses' station. Let's try to do this as soon as we can. It's going to be a long shift; I'm not even sure what that means."

Alina got into some clean scrubs; washed her face and masked up. She wanted to gain some administrative skills but didn't plan on it being like this. Not seeing all the charts or having that meeting, as she walked around, she briefed those in the ER to triage, and she would do her best to work through patients. That was a start.

They had airlifted the mother and baby out to another facility. That opened two more spaces in the ICU. There were at least a half a dozen people in the waiting room. She was doing the mental math and deciding on the fly how to organize. The day receptionists and office people would not be on in the evening; they would have one night person at that desk. There were two aides, an LPN, and only one RN for the overnight. Cami had already started her second shift, taking the place of another nurse who had called in earlier.

"Help! Help! I need help. My son, he's not breathing. Please!"

The woman was hysterical, trying to carry her young son and almost falling. An aide grabbed her in time. Alina knew who the first patient was.

Walking and talking, "I'm Dr. Levin. Can you tell me what's been going on?"

Alina was questioning and examining the child at the same time. An urgency ensued; Cami got the vitals. The mother composed herself. Alina noted labored respiration. There was a temperature but, in a moment, a seizure occurred and moved things along. Quickly, Alina medicated the young boy for the seizure. He relaxed, and his breathing was more normal. This was a very sick boy.

When the immediate emergency subsided, there was no slowdown! She could only talk to the mother briefly. The boy had been feeling off for a couple of days. They hoped it was just a cold or a flu bug. They tested for Covid; he came up positive. In another cubicle, a broken leg had been waiting. The gentleman was in pain and growing more impatient. He was probably in his sixties and was hanging decorative lights around the porch for the coming holiday weekend when he fell. Though there were several other accidents, the number of Covid intakes was growing. More than half of the people Alina saw had the virus. She was grateful a few were not so ill and weren't admitted. The hospital was filling up, which reminded her to think of what to do next if they needed beds.

She stood quietly, then leaned on the desk for a quick break. An aide, Mrs. James, who had worked there for a long time, said she had made fresh coffee and brought some sweet bread in when she came on shift. She encouraged Alina to grab a few minutes' rest. It shocked the aide when she found out from the others that this was the young doctor's third shift.

"Lina, Alina!" Cami was shaking her.

"Okay, okay! Where to next? I'm okay."

She heard Cami say, "Really?"

When her eyes focused, Alina saw the smile of the nurse, who was a good friend and a great colleague. "You've been resting for about 15 minutes. It's almost morning. Dr. Stone will be in soon, and Anne Riley-Ward will come in the afternoon and early evening. I don't know what happens after that, but we need to get some actual sleep so we can at least think. Oh, Dr. Keeler will come for a short while, sometime. That's not firmed up. Today was his day off, but he knows the situation."

"Sounds hopeful," was all that Alina could manage. Then she remembered. Mrs. Scott, one of the hospital administrators who might help with more beds!

"I had an idea. The ICU is filling up. They have postponed most elective surgeries, especially with the numbers surging. Maybe the ambulatory or day patients wing? It's an isolated area. I know it only has four beds, but it could be a real asset."

"Sounds like a plan. Go home. Mrs. Scott isn't here yet. I'm not sure if she will come in. You can call in to talk to someone later, after you get some rest."

"What about Gabe?"

"I haven't heard about him either."

Looking distracted, Alina said, "I will get some rest, but there is one more thing, Delia." Cami could see there would be no dissuading her. Alina was already heading down the hall. She approached the door, turning in to see how her oldest patient was doing. Sadly, there wasn't any apparent change and as she had said so many times before, at least she wasn't worse. She grabbed her hand. It was as if she were sleeping. Vitals were good, no fever. Thinking out loud, "If you could just wake up! I get it. Everything's pressing in on you."

It was ever so slight. Alina wasn't even sure it had happened, but she felt Delia squeeze her hand. *My imagination? I'm tired.* She checked her vitals; nothing seemed to change. Everything was in place and working. But... she couldn't shake it. Something. There was something.

"You haven't left yet?"

It was Cami. She wondered what was going on. Alina seemed distressed. She was beyond spent after three shifts. Everyone was giving over 100%. The staff was small under normal circumstances. These were far from normal times. Now it was unreal. It could be a problem to even keep the hospital open. Then what? So many people need help of all kinds, never mind the ones with chronic issues.

"I would have sworn that she squeezed my hand. It wasn't random; I was feeling sorry for myself and talking to her. Imagine that. This woman is unconscious, and I'm talking to her."

Cami followed but questioned, "It was an involuntary muscle movement. You know that. Right?"

All Alina could say was, "It didn't seem that way."

You could see her frustration and concern. "Maybe we can work on weaning her off the tube. Delia hasn't had any more seizures; the temp is down, and she has been resting. I wish Gabe or Dr. Keeler were on so we could discuss this. It's proven to be a fragile situation, but the longer they're intubated, the chances of coming off continue to diminish."

"I know that," was Cami's reply. "But you need to go home now while you can. It's been over 36 hours; go home. Plan to do something next shift and hopefully, there will be more staff back over the next few days. Plus, you need to talk to her family first. Go home and get some rest."

She knew Cami was right. It wasn't a hard procedure, but she was depleted. There was a skeleton crew, and it is a procedure that can go wrong and have unexpected consequences. She would need to talk to the family. They call in every day but often talk to the charge nurse since there are only a few doctors available to the entire hospital. At least, that's how it was lately.

"Okay. I need to get sleep, or I won't be good to anyone. I am going to check in on Gabe, though."

As she went through the front doors of the hospital and out to the parking lot, the fresh air was welcome. Alina took a deep breath and felt herself more invigorated, which was good since she had to drive to Gabe's and then home. She pulled out of the lot and did a quick trip up to the drive through at a Tim Horton's, which would cover coffee, sandwiches, and soup. The intention was to bring the soup and sandwiches to Gabe, and she needed something, too.

Hard to believe it had been 36 hours since she had been home. Her neighbors were a blessing and took care of Jax when work was over the top. Alina had rented their carriage house. The home was Victorian style, with about three acres of land just on the outskirts of town. She felt as if she'd found a jewel when first seeing the place, and it proved to be just that. They had an eleven-year-old son who loved Jax almost as much as she did. This was also a blessing because a resident's schedule is anything but regular. The move into this small town was as smooth as any move across the country could be. She was grateful it had turned out this well, especially with the events of the pandemic. There was a sign as you drove into the town: Hillstown, A Good Place to Live. This was a familiar sign throughout the state, referring to whatever place you were entering. It was true here.

Gabe lived a few blocks in the opposite direction. She parked and gathered the food she had picked up. Knocking twice brought him to the door. He looked worn out. Gesturing with the free arm, she greeted him. She masked, trying to follow procedures, especially since they were both doctors, and the staffing impact was concerning.

Alina spoke first. "You're looking under it. How's it going?"

"Thanks, I guess," was Gabe's reply with a wry smile. "I'm doing better. No temp for the last day and a half. I've been sleeping better. I'm fatigued but aiming to get back in another day or two."

"Have you been eating?" Gabe rolled his eyes. "Some. I really like Tim Horton's."

"Glad you do. I'll try to bring something else tomorrow. I'm off. Had to do three shifts."

Gabe's eyes widened. "What? Three?"

"The staff is exhausted. We've had so many call in; others are coming in and working that same way. There's no recovery."

"Like you?"

She smiled and said, "Well, whatever. Get sleep. I intend to. I'll call, or you can call me if you need anything."

Gabe thanked her. Alina headed out the door and into the car. She needed rest, and now.

Day 8

Alina opened her eyes and felt refreshed. Not ready to do another 36 hours, but better and more alert than yesterday. The weather was decent, and it helped. Amazing what a little sleep will do for your outlook. She made coffee and went back to bed. Her window looked to the east over a small, beautiful garden. Jax was happy on the edge of the bed. There was a sweet peace. She could stay there, maybe not forever, but for a long time.

It was only her third month at the hospital; she was feeling settled despite the unsettled atmosphere. If things were different, she might even feel confident in the new residency, but the reach of the pandemic was beyond what anyone could have expected. Enough of what could have been. Heading out to the park seemed like a good idea, but not just yet. Not having to go anywhere for a while was very appealing.

* * *

Delia sat on the edge of the bed wondering how she could even write to Mike. Here they were on opposite ends of the world, or at least that's what it felt like. She had the most important thing to tell her husband, and she couldn't even get through with a phone call. A letter was it! She struggled. Nausea struck again. A mad dash to the bathroom followed. She felt better once that had happened. The queasiness subsided. The doctor had said after the first trimester, things should be better. That was something to look forward to. She only planned to close her eyes for a minute or two. Hearing the phone startled her, and she looked at her watch. More than an hour passed. How could anyone ever get anything done like this? It was still ringing. Reaching the bottom of the stairs, she grabbed the phone. It was Aunt Janie checking on her and letting her know she would bring dinner... again. Delia wanted to fight it, but that was useless. Plus, Janie was an excellent cook. If she had to eat, she might as well enjoy it.

There was time to write.

Dear Mike, that just didn't sound right. Dear! Not how they talked. It was as if they were forty or more. Maybe how their parents or grandparents would talk, but not them. Just *Mike.*

I've struggled with a letter and I'm so sorry I fainted and made us miss the call, so we're stuck with this. I'm thinking about you all the time, hoping to hear from you soon. It's hard to wait; I thought I would write first. I need to write. The last three months have been a roller coaster. So much has happened and now... well, I have something to tell you. We're going to have a baby! I didn't want it to be like this. We should be together. I want to see your face. But it's not to be. I'm okay.

That's what the fainting was about, at least part of it. I hadn't eaten much over the last few days. The whole family, including Aunt Janie, is on it. There's more food in the house than I've ever seen. I guess that's good. People at work have been very supportive. I'm not unhappy about the baby, just wish you were here. Love.

That was the best she could do. She wasn't happy or confident about anything. Who would be?

* * *

Alina called in to the hospital to check on her patients, the man with the broken leg, several Covid patients and, of course, Delia.

"Any changes?"

"No, Doctor Levin. Nothing to report either way. I suppose that's good."

"It can be, for the moment. We have enough people in crisis."

Again, she entertained the idea it was time to discuss weaning Delia off the ventilator. The nurse gave her Karen's home number; she would call tonight. All the everyday things waited, regardless of how busy the hospital was. You still had laundry, groceries, and bills. She filled today with the mundane business of life. Pulling into her driveway, she took a breath. For a moment, she was too tired to get out of the car. One night's sleep didn't do it. Alina laughed at the possibilities of that scene. A headline could read *Local Doctor Found Unconscious in Car.* Enough of that, and the timing was perfect. The Johnson's son, Billy, came out the door with Jax, tail wagging, making a speed run toward her. That was the best greeting, and she needed it now. 3 shifts! 36 plus hours had extended effects. There was a hope that would not become a regular thing, but fear arose it might well be. Shake off that thought. She thanked Billy for all his help and hauled the groceries, the dog, dry cleaning, and an assortment of odds and ends into the cottage. When Billy headed out, she looked around, and it seemed like an insurmountable collection of stuff that needed attention. There was no energy; *too bad it couldn't all put itself away at the snap of a finger.* She laughed. The rest of the day dragged on with a battle between how she felt and what needed to be done. In the hospital she had to keep going, but at home, not so much. If things didn't get done, she was getting better at accepting they didn't get done. Though this wasn't the ideal choice, she put what needed to be refrigerated away and let the rest go. It felt good.

Evening came quickly on this feel-good day. Alina had to get back to her work mode. Using a telehealth appointment, she called Delia's daughter. With all the restrictions, these appointments gave a family or patient more personal attention.

That was important in building confidence and extending compassion in these challenging times. She introduced herself again, assuring Karen that there was no emergency. Quite the contrary. She noted that Delia's condition was stable, and she was resting comfortably. The young doctor related her concerns about any patient staying on a ventilator for extended periods.

"I think Delia's a good choice for trying to wean off the ventilator. It can be a serious decision. I can't promise there won't be a problem."

Karen asked, "What can happen if she's not ready?"

That was a fair question and expected. "I wish I could have a definite answer, but I don't. The best case is she would start breathing on her own with some help. That's the idea. We are using a new oxygenation method known as HFNO, High-flow nasal oxygen therapy. This therapy can generate low-level positive airway pressure. It reduces airway resistance and washes out nasopharyngeal dead space. Other hospitals have been trying this with virus patients with some success; we would like to try it with Delia."

Karen looked apprehensive. Anyone making this kind of decision would. She asked the question.

"What if it doesn't work?"

"That would depend on Delia and the reaction she has. If she had to go back on the ventilator, that would not be the best outcome. You can think about it. I want to be sure we plan, and I want at least one or two of my colleagues to be present. When I left the other day, more staff had Covid. I want to have the best scenario in place to do this because I am not convinced continuing on the ventilator is the best path for Delia."

Alina preferred talking face to face; this was the quickest way to plant the idea and maybe get things in motion. Staffing is a problem. A small hospital with several staff out doesn't have the coverage it should, to monitor the way a city hospital can. She felt hesitation in Karen's lack of response and encouraged her to think about it. She didn't have to respond now, but the young doctor said not to wait too long. With that, the conversation ended, and Alina was back to her day off, a little less relaxed. She knew the risks either way, but thought it was time to try.

* * *

Delia slept through the night. She planned to go back to work in the morning, but hadn't let herself think about it, or she wouldn't have slept. She dreaded facing everyone, but knew once she got past the first hour, it would be fine. Ella was there to greet her and sincerely gushed with concern. Delia reassured her she felt much better and rested. One by one, including her boss, Mr. Wells, came to welcome her back. How could they be so nice? Truthfully, these people were nice. Delia was a hard worker, and even though she had been there only a short time, was punctual and did more than expected. When so many only did what was necessary, she was a model employee. Mr. Wells knew the story and understood the young couple would need the money Delia was bringing home. He had a plan to stagger her hours, cutting back a little when needed but allowing for some flexibility. She was very grateful and relaxed, looking at the new routine as helpful.

Before heading to work, she had dropped the letter off at the post office. It was done. That's about how she felt. What should have been a joy wasn't even close. Delia had done her best to sound assured, happy, and in control. All of which were far from the truth. It wasn't about the baby. This was their baby, her's and Mike's, a part of them, and would be loved by them and the extended family. Her only anger was about this ridiculous war. The most frustrating part was the protesting. She wanted to protest too, but the protesters even went after the soldiers who came home, as if any of them were happy about what was going on. Maybe there were some who were career military, but they're not the ones deciding and sending 18-year-olds overseas. If she was going to stay sane, she had to focus on her family. That was enough, all she could handle. She wasn't even sure she was handling it.

A few days passed, and she was looking for something, a response, a letter; Delia knew that was impossible, but still hoped. Each day ran into the next. She was doing well at work and felt a little less nauseous, which was very welcome. No one would know from her appearance, but she was changing, almost a size larger. The last few months were more unnerving than anyone could imagine, unless you lived them as she, Mike, and the family had. She was the youngest in the office, and the staff had a paternal/maternal kind of thing going on. Again, this was almost a hidden blessing. Other places of employment, such as the bigger chain stores, couldn't possibly have that atmosphere.

More time passed. There was no information, and Mike was away for about a month now, not counting his training. It was becoming worrisome.

Delia didn't know much about Viet Nam or Cambodia. The only thing she could think of when it came up were the jungles or small villages. That's how the news would describe the countries day after day. It was a new generation, watching war on TV as it was going on, not exactly in real time, but current events and videos seemed unreal. She wished a letter would come and had even tried the support group at the base. It was a drive to get there; plus, she was never much on groups, but it was helpful to hear about others who were in the same position. They knew the ropes and filled her in on what happens when and who she could contact if she needed to talk to someone. When the units were out on a mission, it could be a while before you heard anything. Add to that, these guys were new, with significant travel ahead of them to their camps in the field. Some would receive updated training. Leaders would explain the typical day-to-day things about mail and their missions. Everything took time. Also, it was not out of the question, the Viet Cong would disrupt communications. There were so many variables.

Distraction was the path to peace and sanity. Work and family were the biggest distractions now. There was a comfort in living in her home with her father and brothers. Aunt Janie was a regular and the mother she didn't have. People surrounded her with kindness and support. She didn't want that from them or anyone in the beginning. Everything changed. How relieved she felt now.

Day 9

Alina parked the car and headed to the front doors of the hospital. Other than immediate emergency situations, these were the only doors they were using right now. It was easier to keep track of people, be sure everyone had a mask if needed, and take temperatures. One door was a solution.

Sleep helped. You see things in a different light, more positively, when you don't feel overwhelmed. The concern was how long would her current sense of well-being last?

"Good morning!" The young doctor greeted everyone at the nurses' station. Hard to see smiles with the masks, but no furrowed lines on foreheads or telltale eyebrows raised by her comments. Maybe a good sign?

"Good morning, Dr. Levin. How are you doing?"

"Cami, you here? I'm feeling well. How has everything been? Is there another doctor on today?"

Cami laughed and said, "I'm well. I took one day. Dr. Keeler came in a little while ago. Doctor Stone was here last night and needed a break since he came directly from his clinic before that."

"I gather things are a struggle as far as staff."

"We haven't seen too big an increase in the numbers, so we're holding. But it hasn't been easy. It's a fragile situation.

A lot of sick people came through the ER. Fortunately, most went home. We used the ambulatory area for more beds, and that nurse practitioner, Anne Riley-Ward, came for part of a shift. She's great and a big help. We're holding. That's the best I can say."

"Well, truthfully, that's better than I could have expected. You listen to the news and things just seem to get worse. So, I'm happy we're holding. How's Delia doing?"

"She's stirred a few times. Not seeming too stressed or in any significantly different medical situation. Yesterday, I almost felt like she was awake or coming to, but she settled. Everything seems steady."

Cami's response was what Alina wanted to hear. Steady was good. Almost waking up, good as well. That Doctor Keeler was in, another plus! She asked about the other patients she had seen her last shift; they had discharged some and kept others. This was also good news. The bad news... the sick were coming in and any beds they had gained filled quickly. Alina thought *not a horrible report.* After reading the notes, she headed to Delia's room. Dr. Keeler was passing by in the hall and saw Alina and stopped in.

"Just the man I wanted to see."

"I'm not sure if that's good or bad," was the response. Dr. Keeler was affable and a hard worker. Beyond that, he was a good doctor with common sense. Alina was building her case for extubating Delia. Her lungs sounded better, not perfect, but better. The young resident had already reduced her sedation, which she had prescribed to keep her calm and to offset any stress from the intubation. She kept some in place with the uncertainty of the situation. Now it was 9 days, which, according to some studies, was a turning point for patient evaluation. Dr. Keeler was supportive of Alina's assessment. She informed him that Delia's children were now on board, nervous, but on board. The doctors reduced the level of oxygen and observed Delia's reaction and vitals. Alina was hopeful because her overall presentation was stable, and sedation was at a much lower dose. When Delia came in, she was sick and struggling, but not at the most critical levels. Considering these factors resulted in the decision to start a weaning trial.

It was the beginning of Alina's shift, so she would be here to assess Delia every step of the way. Hope and confidence rose. It was about time for Delia to move forward. She would call Karen and give her the details of the plan. Alina knew the importance of keeping the family updated and addressing questions. This was their mother.

* * *

It was over a week, and Delia hadn't heard anything. Mr. Wells had come up with flex hours for some employees who needed a more fluid work schedule. They took a little less pay but kept their jobs. Several new individuals chose this plan. It was more than part-time, but slightly less than full-time. Today, Delia would go in late morning. She was moving a little slower these days, not because her pregnancy advanced, but simply because she was tired. She felt bone tired. That was an expression her father would use. She smiled and laughed almost. Must be getting old.

She thought she heard a car pull up, but dismissed it and finished combing her hair. Her father called, and turning, she headed down the stairs. Delia stopped on the landing. Everything stopped. Two uniformed men were in the hallway with her father. He extended his hand, and she ignored it, almost instinctively. The lack of response might forestall what she sensed was coming. How could it be?

They apologized and relayed that Michael Parker had fallen in combat and it was with regret that they brought this news. She and the family would be proud that he had served with honor and saved several members of his platoon. There was more, but it dragged off. She didn't faint but didn't respond and put her hand on the railing to steady herself. Her father was speaking to the men, and they left. She didn't know what to do. A numbness came over her like everything was out of focus, surreal.

What should have been the best time of their lives wasn't; now her life was wrong, broken. Her father had been talking the whole time. Trying to guide her from the landing steps to the sofa in the living room. She couldn't seem to move in any direction.

Day 10

Alina had talked to Karen again, letting her know that Dr. Keeler agreed, and they had prepared Delia, reducing her oxygen and sedation. They would do the Spontaneous Breathing Trial, which was periodic testing to see how Delia might do on her own. Again, Alina wanted to stress it was a gradual process to determine if Delia was ready.

Delia's vitals were stable. The chest congestion was minimal. There had been a couple of seizures in the very beginning, and the congestion and temperatures would come and go. These subsided and were not occurring to the degree they had been. Originally, they sedated and intubated to support her breathing and reduce the incidence of seizures. Now it was day 10. Delia had times when she was lucid but weak. There was never a fight or struggle. Over recent days, it appeared she was less stressed and congestive. The young doctor was very determined. It was time to get her off the vent. Delia didn't seem stressed by the decreased oxygen, a good sign. Alina asked Cami and the shift nurses to watch her closely; this would be a brief experiment to test the situation. They would check her every 15 minutes. She would try to see some patients, but be back in about 40 minutes. They could page her if anything happened.

After checking in on the other patients, she made her way back to the nurses' station. They hadn't paged her, so that was good. Bob Street, one of the nurses, greeted her and let her know Delia seemed to tolerate the lower dose of oxygen well. She was semi-conscious. "What?" This got Alina's attention. Street said there were a few times when she tried to open her eyes. With that, Alina was on the way to Delia's room.

Cami was there, checking everything. When Alina approached the bed briefly, Delia opened her eyes. With that, the young woman greeted her, saying hello. The old woman's eyes were struggling to focus. After all the time that passed, it was not uncommon. There was a pause as she looked at Alina; then closed them again. But for that moment... Alina couldn't shake the eyes.

She called Dr. Keeler in, and they decided to extubate Delia. The circumstances were as good as they would get. Tim had a lot of questions and was more reluctant than his sister, Karen. Both could see the situation could not go on forever, and the dangers would only increase with time on the ventilator. The process did not take long, and it wasn't complicated. Patients may cough. Some may panic. The goal was to keep it smooth and do it quickly but carefully.

Delia struggled, and there was a panic on her face. Alina kept reassuring her that everything was fine. Breathe slowly.

Then, almost breathing with her, Alina coached, "Steady! Slowly!" She sprinkled encouraging words in with directions.

After a few minutes, it was easy to see Delia was tiring. The eyes fluttered, not dangerously, just with ordinary weariness. At first, the others in the room were concerned about her dropping off, but it was sleep, not a stroke or failure of any sort. Her vitals were fine. It was all a process.

"Okay, we'll keep doing the same thing. She seems to be stable, but we'll need to watch her. Let's do 30 minutes. I'll come back, but one of you should check her every 10. Look at her pulse, respiration, facial appearance. Questions? Page me right away." This was a good start. Alina knew they were in a fragile place, but it was a positive step. She understood today could be fine and tomorrow not so much. At Delia's age and with the illness she experienced, almost 9 full days on a ventilator, they were not out of the woods yet.

The sick kept coming. Some new admittances signaled they were in the thick of it and the end wasn't in sight. It was otherworldly. Parts of the state, New York City, Manhattan, were unbelievable; Queens, the Bronx, were beyond anything Alina would have thought possible. The city was soliciting upstate healthcare workers with very tempting offers. She had received a call last week with a job offer from a renowned Manhattan hospital. They would move her; provide an advance with a salary she would have only dreamed about. When she considered it, *simply not a chance!*

Some think this far upstate is the woods! Who would even want to be in a place like this? The edge of nowhere! The boonies! It didn't take her long. Alina decided plainly. *Here to stay!* She would make that same decision again and again. There were people who needed care; this was an underserved population. The pace was active enough for a relatively new doctor. There were horror stories of interns and even medical students going to the downstate city hospitals. Covid overwhelmed the facilities and their staffing. That was a story Alina didn't want to be part of, though she admired those who went. She was happy where she was and moved on with her rounds. There were a few more admissions since she came in. ICU was full, but the ambulatory wing beds had helped. They were coping, hard to say for how long.

When she returned to the ICU, everything was as she had left it. The nurses' reports on Delia were positive. She wasn't awake, but she wasn't struggling. For the time being, Alina would take that as a good sign.

* * *

Things slowed down. It was surreal. A feeling overtook her like water, the way it would in the ocean, weightless but bringing resistance. When you're under, you're free but enveloped. Every emotion brushed over her; and people were trying to be considerate, comforting. Nothing worked. How could it? She wanted them to go away but didn't. She couldn't think clearly. *What do I do now? What about the baby? Where should I live? The funeral?* That last one... the hardest to think about. She couldn't plan. Not that.

The men left after they got her settled. She didn't appear heavily pregnant, but her father had told them. It started. The looks of pity; the comments about how sorry everyone was; Right! Standard comments. How could anyone understand? She didn't understand. Things were spinning whether her eyes were open or closed. Just when she was moving out of the first trimester, and it was supposed to get better. This. The fuzziness passed. The weight of it didn't.

Her father spoke first. "Delia, I'm so sorry. I know that isn't much. I don't know what to say or do. If I could change it, I would. I wasn't for the marriage because you were so young, but he was a great guy. I never questioned his character, and I guess he proved that true with the people he saved."

His words drifted; she was aware but not focused, or responsive. What parent doesn't want to comfort their child? Child. She and Mike would have a child. He would never see the baby or hold it, but it was his child. How could she do this? Having a baby and being apart was enough. But it allowed her to think about when Mike came home. That was different and the key to walking through the time she was waiting. *Mike was coming home.*

He was coming home, but not the way she hoped. This news, this day, had lurked in her from the beginning. Oh, it wasn't some spooky foreshadowing; reality was all around them. Family upon family had faced a day like today. It was her turn.

"Delia, Delia," her father's voice vied for the attention of the other voices playing out in her head. He encouraged her to get some rest. "We'll figure out what to do. You're not alone." She didn't respond out loud, but heard in her head. *I don't think I can rest.*

Day 11

Alina was doggedly tired. Things at the hospital were better than she thought they would be, which is good, but didn't change how tired she was. Knowing that they had taken steps with Delia, and she seemed to continue to be stable, was an encouragement to everyone. For Alina, there was something about her. Not that there had been much interaction. But her eyes... so expressive, especially that one time. As she approached the nurse's station, it appeared the floor was quiet with no incidents or admits. That lasted for about five minutes.

The ER called up. There was an accident just outside of town, a head on collision that caught a third vehicle in the mix. It was serious. So much for the quiet night. She called for Cami and asked if Dr. Keeler was here and to give Gabe a call. He thought he would come back tomorrow. She was pushing it, but They were going to need help. So, maybe. There was one other nurse left on the floor. She had four patients. That was about the extent of it before any of these new incoming.

Everyone sprang into motion as the ambulances rolled in. The skill of those with whom she was working always impressed her. All the EMTs focused steely on the injured; one was critical; three others sustained injuries from cuts and scrapes to open wounds and breaks. It would be a busy shift.

Families of the victims arrived within the hour, directed by the police and hospital staff. After about forty-five minutes, the chaos passed. The critical patient was stable. The others, when cleaned up, had injuries but were less concerning. ICU was full. There were no more beds. A small alcove at the end of the hall in the ER wing had an area where they could set up a couple of beds, maybe even three. After that, Alina did not know what to do next. Delia!

She cleaned herself up and headed into Delia's room. The older woman was resting. Pulse and respiration were good. Her chest wasn't 100% clear, but acceptable for the moment. They were waiting for her eyes to open and hoping that would be soon. No temperature and no other seizures. Both elements were positive. Things had settled; she enjoyed the moment. The silence was therapeutic.

"Hello." A familiar voice drew her attention. It was Gabe.

She smiled in response and stepped toward the door and joined her colleague in the hallway.

"Thank you!"

"For what?" was the genial reply.

"Are you kidding? For coming in. I don't know how we would have gotten through the last couple of hours without you."

"Good enough," was his answer. "I'm not contagious; yes, I'm tired, but that goes with the territory. With you and Keeler and that NP, we're surviving."

"Yeah, barely." Alina looked with raised eyebrows.

He asked if she wanted to catch something to eat, and that gained another side glance. There was no cafeteria. He related he would pick something up from down the street. The break room was empty. Alina laughed, "Why not?"

When Gabe ran out for food, she would do a quick once around. When she looked in again at Delia, the woman's eyes were open. She approached the bed and smiled. Putting her hand on the old woman's arm, she said, "It's good to see your eyes open. We've been waiting for you. The hospital doesn't allow visitors now, but I have been in contact with Karen and Tim. They've been waiting."

Delia's brow furrowed. She tried to touch her throat and seemed distressed, shaking her head ever so slightly.

Alina understood. "You feel as if your throat hurts? That's normal. It will pass. We're going to take it easy."

Recognition was in her eyes. No movement or response, but an awareness. She could see frustration. Delia blinked, then stared right at her. Alina had her hand on her patient's arm. The old woman almost raised a finger, to reach, or a question, but then began looking to her side and closing her eyes again.

This didn't seem stressful. The numbers didn't change. No emergency was imminent; she was tired. Even though it was awkward, Alina felt that this was an acceptable beginning. It convinced her Delia was lucid, just weak. She updated the nurses. Only a few minutes later, and Gabe was back. He remembered the other staff and brought some snacks and coffee for them.

They gratefully dove in and appreciated their colleague's thoughtfulness, which went a long way in these tense times. Everyone seized the moment, enjoying the peace for however long it would last.

Day 12

The following days seemed to pass without her participation. Delia only did what she had to do. The Parkers came over. Grief overwhelmed them with the loss of their only son. It robbed all the joy that would follow a wedding and impending grandchild. Delia's father and Aunt Janie took the lead, and everyone let them. It was a military funeral on a small scale. The funeral was simple. They honored him as a veteran and a hero. Only the immediate families and a few friends attended. For that, Delia was grateful. It was hard even limited to this small group. The Parkers had a meal back at their home. The setting was comforting, but emotional. Scattered pictures of happier times filled the house. Delia didn't want to look up or talk with anyone, but she went through the motions. These were family who cared for them; each had stepped up in their own way with time, gifts, and support. She was doing her best, praying it would end soon.

It did. By mid to late afternoon, she headed back home. All that she wanted was to sleep and forget, at least for a little while. And that's all it was... a little while. She heard tapping on her door. It took everything to get up. It was an official letter from the government. Finn saw that and thought it might be important. At another time, she might have thought so. It was about benefits, how to apply, what was available. Again, not today. Delia knew the importance of getting things in order. With the baby, paying attention to all the incoming information was critical. The baby.

She got her wish and woke up around 10:00 **PM**. That was the most sleep she had gotten in a while and had to admit, it helped. All of it was terrible, but sleep makes functioning more doable. Functioning was the goal. Taking care of business, going to work, taking care of herself, life was about each of those things.

* * *

With the break in the patient flow and something to eat, the staff felt invigorated. Everyone was tired, but even the brief rest and food helped. More than a few were on a second shift, or some with no days off over the last week; they were not foolish enough to think they could sustain the calm, but it was a pleasant hope. They coveted even minutes of rest.

Over the next week, the Covid patients increased. They were heading into the fall. Anticipating more inside gatherings, especially with school reopening, the staff was concerned. They were holding on by a thread. There was little else to do but take one day at a time. With shortages of everything all over, from medical supplies to staff and everyday goods, people were on edge. For a rural area, shortages of the basics could become even more dire. Alina wanted to be in a place that was underserved, and she was.

After her shift, the park was on the list. When she had little time, it was on the list. There was a simple beauty there that offered a great transition to finding that rest. Jax loved it, too. And who wouldn't trust Jax? A smile came over her. This was the right decision. The Adirondacks were a unique place, but she learned not to mention winter again; that had been a mistake.

When you're single, you go through stages creating how you want to live: neat, messy, collector, or minimalist? Sometimes, you're in a fierce mood to cook and wildly overdo it. Usually, that's followed by an undetermined period of junk food. It's hard to figure life out. For a while, Alina wasn't even trying. School, the internship, even applications for residency demanded every ounce of strength and attention. Now those were in the past. The new life, even during the pandemic with all its oddities, was leaving spaces. For what?

Her beeper went off, and she wasn't ready for what the emergency was. In her mind, at the top of the list, was Delia, but the emergency was something she never expected. It was Gabe.

"I'll be there in 15 minutes." She needed to get Jax home and head over to the hospital. The good thing about living near the hospital was just that. She was near the hospital. Her mind was racing. With Jax settled, she grabbed her keys and hurried out. Plowing through the doors, Cami met her on her way into the ER.

"He collapsed. Everything was fine. Rounds ended. He conferred with a few people about patients and while he was doing notes, he just collapsed at the nurses' station."

By the time she got to the ER, there were people both in the room and spilling out the doorway into the hallway. Dr. Stewart was resting. The chaos of the moment had passed. The ER was quieter, and the staff was waiting. Alina quickly realized she was in charge. Anne Ward, the NP, was with Gabe; beyond that there were only two other doctors, and they were not present. Though it functioned as a hospital, Community General was small, more like a larger clinic with beds.

Alina moved through the onlookers, her nerves pumping. This was Gabe. Vitals were good, steady considering he passed out. She asked if they checked his blood sugar. They did, and it was low. Anne Ward said it was a quick event; he seemed to drop, almost fold over. No temp, nothing obvious, no pain or rashes. She felt he had come back too soon from Covid. Even though he had tested negative and been home for several days, the stress and pace of events at the hospital were not normal. He was on a normal shift that was far from ordinary.

Alina said she would stay, at least for a while. Cami spoke up and said that Delia was awake. With that, she headed down the hall. The old woman's eyes fixed on Alina as she entered the room and greeted her. The woman looked with concern and surprised the doctor when she touched her arm. Their eyes locked, and Delia spoke.

"Doc... Doctor" This caught Alina's attention. She lifted her lower arm an inch or two and seemed to point to the hallway with a slight nod. Cami had said there was a lot of commotion when Gabe passed out. The staff came from every direction to the nurses' station.

"Yes, Doctor Stewart. I think he'll be okay. He had Covid and returned to work before he fully had his strength back. I'm confident he'll be okay."

"Ga..."

"Gabe, that's him!" Alina could see the concern on Delia's face. Her thoughts couldn't help but take this as very encouraging. The woman didn't have the strength or voice to do or say much, but the fact she was aware and tried speaking was so vitally important.

She spent a few minutes talking to Delia, assessing her, and left the room satisfied. Alina promised the staff another six hours, which they gratefully appreciated, since Anne Ward would leave shortly. As she walked down the hallway, Alina felt she was coming down from an adrenaline high. That surprised her. Though she was young, she was not new to emergencies, not here or anywhere. In Texas, she spent her internship and other training time in a large urban hospital. Often, those settings were continuously fast paced and high powered; the reason for looking for a different location was to find a place where she could have more time with patients. Emergencies didn't throw her; it was the desire to not run from one to the next constantly. Though she didn't readily admit it, this emergency wasn't the problem. It was Gabe. At first, Alina wanted to dismiss it. That wasn't as simple as it sounded in her head. She hadn't let herself think that something might develop between them. It was too soon. A new chapter in her life was just beginning and made more complicated under the umbrella of the pandemic. Effectively, she blocked it out, but that didn't mean the awareness went away.

* * *

Tomorrow, Delia would return to work. Everyone said to take more time and how she needed it, but they couldn't imagine sitting at home all day and doing what? What she needed was her husband, the father of her baby. That would not happen. Why sit at home? At least at work, after the initial return, she could do something. People would eventually stop bringing it up. Work was busy but peaceful. They were a small office supply company and even managed a temporary worker's service. Consultations were available for products and evaluations of a company's efficiency. Mr. Wells was a smart man. He stayed in his lane and didn't let things get out of hand or too big. His business was helping small businesses. He wasn't old, though Delia had thought of him that way; Wells was probably fiftyish. When you're eighteen, that's old. She prepped herself for the stares, as she would return to her job and the community. That was the part she hated. The looks of pity and awkwardness as people wondered what to say to the poor, pregnant eighteen-year-old widow. That word was the worst.

Fighting her father's pleading, she went to work. There were some awkward exchanges, as expected. They passed. She did mostly clerical things and regular office tasks, such as answering phones or making calls. It felt like solid ground. That's what she needed now. Solid ground. Only five months had passed since the letter that started the young couple down the path she could never have imagined. Taking a deep breath, she felt she was moving forward, at least with work.

When she got home, her father was calm. He could see she was okay. Compared to every other day lately, it was a blessing. He relaxed when Delia had dinner and sat in the living room for a while watching TV. Normal. It was welcome. Even the family struggled with what to say and do. As they watched the evening news, it was hard to escape the Viet Nam war; when her brothers were with their friends, it was a hot topic with words always flying in every direction. They would bring news of the discussions, especially if someone enlisted or was called up. When the TV came on, or they talked about these events, there were always instances of awareness or apology. Something else she got used to. A silence fell. They would plod through the awkwardness. No matter, she loved her family and was very grateful for them. What would she have done without them?

A routine developed. Routines can be tiresome, but are not always bad. Work filled out her life. It made it easy. There were no big decisions, and everyone knew what to do and what their boundaries were, which made for a peaceful atmosphere. The business prospered; that was no surprise to Delia. Mr. Wells was a skilled manager. In fact, they needed to take on a couple of new people. One was a young girl around Delia's age. When she saw her come in on the first day, there was a familiarity about her. Within a couple of weeks, they had brief conversations. These were small communities. You would know many people just by their appearance. The girls didn't know each other from school. A connection came through church, and it was quite a few years back. Delia's mom was a faithful member of a local church community. The girls had been in classes together and attended a variety of picnics, bazaars, and bake sales. Sara was easygoing and a good worker. She didn't ask a lot of questions. They reminisced, talked about work and friends they might have in common. She still attended that church, which was on the main road between Harrison's Landing and Hillstown. Every now and again, Sara would invite Delia, but the time hadn't come when she felt comfortable enough to accept. Her world was small-family and work; now she had a friend. She never really had a lot of friends because her family was large, and the girl cousins were more like friends. They did everything together. Times changed when they graduated. Some cousins were older, working and even starting families; others closer to Delia's age were in college. Sara was following what had been Delia's original plan. Attend college locally and save money working part time.

She was an easy friend to have, affable and nonintrusive. Most were aware of Delia's background, and Sara never pushed with questions, but didn't treat her as fragile. Delia's pregnancy would have eliminated the majority of girls in her age bracket. Sara was unique. As they got to know each other better, her qualities of kindness and concern would become clear. An unexpected peace and satisfaction came into Delia's life.

* * *

Alina was learning to make the best out of whatever time off came her way. It wasn't easy to adapt sleep patterns, but she knew she had to stay sharp and on top of things. With only four or five doctors in the immediate area and only one or two on staff during a shift, she and the others were trying to take care of themselves. If any of them were out, that would affect the rest.

She needed to pick up groceries. Eating out was becoming too comfortable and wasn't always the best option for healthy living. When you're tired, though, the grocery store is the last place you want to be. With list in hand, Alina entered the store with the intention of it being a quick trip. That was not to be. Emergencies followed her. As she was filling her cart, she heard a noise; maybe cans falling? She saw people running. Screams led her to the aisle where the commotion was. A young pregnant woman was on the floor on her knees, holding her rounded stomach; cans were all over and the makings of a small crowd was gathering. In the cart, next to the woman, sat a toddler who was crying, and his distress was increasing, as was his mother's. Alina opened the conversation with a young woman, who looked up, wincing, and speaking.

"My water broke. I've been having periodic discomfort, but who wouldn't at 36 weeks? The pain has gotten much stronger. I thought it would pass. It did before. I thought they were Braxton Hicks."

"Well, I could see where you might think that, but you're definitely in active labor now." With that, another contraction started verifying that what Alina was saying was true.

"We called for 911, but the truth is you might not make it to the hospital. I think we're going to meet your baby right here."

The doctor asked for towels, directing bystanders to get even small ones from the kitchen display aisle. She followed with a tablecloth. Make it two, packaged would be good, and a pillow if they had one. Luckily, this store had general household items in two of the aisles. The next request was for privacy. One woman stepped up; she was an EMT which was great. A grandmotherly woman from the growing crowd, skilled in baby wrangling, picked up the little boy. The child's emotions were escalating, seeing his mother struggling while leaving him with a stranger. The young woman's husband was in the military, and she said she lived with her mother, who was at work. She barely had the composure to give the contact number, but they got it.

Alina asked that they work on the privacy issue, though the woman was yelling at this point she didn't want to have a baby on the floor of a grocery store. Alina had delivered babies before, but she mentally agreed with the woman. Not like this. She informed her the baby was crowning. Something didn't seem right. She checked again, and the cord had wrapped around the baby's neck. Immediately, she asked the woman to not push; the equally immediate response was, "Are you crazy? I have to push." Firmly, Alina's reply was, "Not now, or you will harm your baby." The woman burst into tears. The EMT tried to calm her and get her to focus on her breathing. This was getting worse by the minute. She held it together, though, and Alina stayed steady and methodically unwound the cord. Within seconds, she said to push and followed with, "You have another handsome son!" His fierce crying told everyone present he was here and strong! The mother was everything you would expect, worn out, relieved, and happy. Alina thanked those who assisted. The EMT took the baby and attended to him. Shortly, he relaxed and was efficiently swaddled in towels. The older woman who was watching the toddler had found a box of animal crackers in the next aisle, so even the distressed toddler had settled. The ambulance arrived, and the paramedics prepared the mother and baby for transport. As they were heading to the front of the store, her mother came through the doors. She joined the scene with equally escalated emotions, but was relieved after taking in her daughter and new grandson. The toddler reached for his grandmother and the craziness dissolved. The crowd extended multitudes of thank-yous to Alina, the EMT, and even the woman who helped with the toddler.

Subsequently, Alina stood in the aisle, alone, then went back to shopping for groceries. She laughed. Contact with people drew her to this area of the country. Surely, she got what she wanted.

Day 13

A good night's sleep changes your perspective. Alina felt re-energized walking into the hospital the next morning. She didn't know what the day would bring, but now her outlook was positive, refreshed even. This was a good start, and she was praying it would last. Smiles greeted her. Another hopeful sign.

"Good morning, Doctor Levin."

The aide behind the nurses' station commented and gave a brief update. She said they were short two nurses but were holding up and got through all the early morning routines.

"How's Dr. Stewart?"

"He had a good night. I think he might leave soon. Dr. Keeler and Nurse Ward thought he was on the mend."

"Good to hear. Did the young woman with the newborn come in okay?"

"Yes, both are fine. We heard what you did. Everyone is talking about it."

Alina smiled and looked down. It was dramatic, if not completely unreal, reminding her of the movie about the baby born in Walmart. Time to move on. Besides these patients, she would also check in on Delia. Let the day begin. Gabe first! As she turned the corner into his room, she didn't see him. That gave her a pause. Then, from the other side of the curtain, a smiling face came.

"You're looking better than the last time I was here."

He was in good spirits, but she could see his tiredness.

"Oh, I've rallied. Will be back to work in no time."

"Whoa, there! That's what got you here. This virus has no mercy. It's rest that you need; maybe a solid week of doing nothing."

"A week! You guys couldn't make it that long without me."

"Well, better a week than another incident that could take you out longer. You know how this goes."

Gabe breathed a deep sigh and tucked his head. He knew he couldn't win.

"Okay, I'm being discharged, though. Doc Stone is coming to pick me up. I'm sure I'll have the same speech from him."

"That's true. How about if I stop by at lunch? I'll bring something. Do a grocery order, and I'll pick it up after I get out later." Looking somewhat sheepish, Gabe replied, "How can I refuse that offer?"

Doctor Stone arrived as planned and took Gabe home. Delia was next in line for a stop. Getting to know people and building relationships were as important as any medicine or treatment. As she walked into the room, a surprise was waiting. Delia was sitting up.

"Well, so great to see you're feeling better."

Alina almost detected a slight smile. The old woman was full of surprises. She struggled, and with a hoarse voice trying to speak, eked out a simple, "Thank you, Doctor." Then the coughing started, and she found it hard to stop. Alina stepped up and gave her some water, instructing her to take little sips. The coughing subsided. Delia looked weary, but when the coughing let up, a weak nod showed she was okay.

"You're doing fine. Take it easy. Recovery is a process and not a fast one. That's the thing everyone is struggling with today. Time. I know it's been a long stretch for you. We all think of you as a miracle. You were very sick. All your prospects are excellent. Let time be a friend, not an enemy."

Her eyes softened. Those eyes. Alina took them in. They spoke volumes; she wished she knew what. Delia insisted with her expression, *how long?* Then, "Home, Home" as plainly as anyone could have spoken. It wasn't said out of fear or depression. Alina responded with a touch to her hand and her voice, "Soon, just keep fighting. You're a warrior!"

She moved on through her day visiting the mom and baby, who were doing well. The ER was busy, but not impossible. There were no critical incidents. Despite all the good, Alina was tired. The last few weeks cut into sleep and relaxation. There isn't compensation or catch up with those elements. We all need consistent doses to function at our best. These were not optimum times to establish those consistencies. It was nearing the end of summer. She understood warm weather could stay through November or snow could arrive much sooner, even crippling snow in late October. When she had made the mistake of bringing up snow, there were nurses who reminisced about Halloween snowstorms, telling how they couldn't make it into work on time. And the eye rolling! She kept the snow to herself now but couldn't help looking forward to it.

At lunch, she had stopped in to drop off a few things for Gabe. She reminded him to call in an order for groceries. She considered that one positive development from the pandemic. Ordering groceries online and picking them up at the curb is perfect when you're not feeling up to shopping or lines. After work, she got them and headed over to Gabe's place. There was a comfort and an ease that was coming into their lives. Alina didn't want to call it a relationship. Of course, they were colleagues, friends, but more? Too soon to even think that, but... When she got to his place, she parked and grabbed the groceries. Gabe opened the apartment door with an affable greeting to let him help. Alina, the independent woman and doctor, said abruptly, "No way! Get back inside. You'll catch cold."

"Cold? 50 degrees is NOT cold! Wait and see what cold really is!" Gabe started laughing.

With that, she handed him the lightest bag, waved her hand to go inside, and picked up the other two bags. The patient relented and turned. She helped him unpack the groceries, and he asked if she wanted to stay for dinner, assuring her he wasn't a bad cook. Her response was simple.

"I'd like to stay, but this has been the craziest week in a long time."

"Oh, you mean the Walmart baby incident?"

Her turn for eyes rolling. "Not you too."

"You're famous," he said with an emerging smirk. "The story keeps growing. You're cool, level-headed, and took command!"

"Enough! The issue is sleep, or lack of sleep. You need to get some good sleep yourself, so you can get back to work so I don't have to deliver more babies in grocery stores. I'll check on you tomorrow."

"Yes, Doctor!"

Shaking her head, Alina went out the door thinking *dinner would have been nice, but there's Jax and I need some serious sleep.*

* * *

Though she was small, she was almost five months pregnant now. Nothing from her closet was making it. Work complicated choices. Larger sized jumpers with tops were her current go to. She let her hair grow out; that simplified things even more. Her appearance was tidy, but when she looked in the mirror, all she would see was a stranger.

Pregnant, no husband and no real life plan. She was in survival mode. There was nothing wrong with that. Surviving was better than the alternative or better than being a simpering wimp swaying in the wind from what others said or offered to do. Ouch! That was harsh, but there were times she surprised herself with how hard and cynical she was becoming. Delia knew this wasn't good but also deep down, knew, or at least hoped, it wasn't true, and it wasn't forever.

She spent a growing amount of time with Sara, who was a comfortable person to be with, a judgment free zone. Everyone needs someone like that. If she wasn't with Sara, she was home. The family had fallen into a peaceful rhythm. They would come home from work; take turns cooking and cleaning up; then head to the living room to watch TV. In another life, that would have gotten to Delia and grown old soon, but after all that had happened, it wasn't so bad. Sitting in the living room with her father and brothers was safe and uncomplicated. She hated the stories about Viet Nam. The emotions were raw, and it wasn't just their family. It seemed as if the country grew in turmoil daily; the rest of what they watched were mindless comedies and variety shows up through the typical medical and police dramas. Delia would doze off, and her father or one of her brothers would gently suggest she should go to bed. Next day, repeat.

After a while, it expectedly grew old, and she reconsidered going to one of the church activities Sara was always pushing. She thought, *I must be getting desperate.* Life can move so slowly, then at other times, the speed of it overwhelms our minds. Right now, it was a slower pace and not unpleasant. The Adirondacks in the fall are beautiful. Delia found comfort in her natural surroundings. She would go to the park. Sitting watching the water or walking around the lake on one of the shorter trails was comforting. There were moments when she felt peace and there were memories, but they didn't seem to hurt the way they used to.

When she got home, her father told her Sara had called and wanted her to call back. For a passing moment, it felt like high school. Girl friends calling in the evening for just about anything, usually gossip. Delia smiled and guessed she wanted to invite her to something... again. *Well, Sara had persistence,* was the thought that came to mind. She took a breath, ate, rested, and got into something comfortable. All the while, she kept trying to come up with yet another excuse not to go to whatever it was Sara was about to put in front of her.

It surprised her. Sara explained about a fall bazaar and festival the church participated in every year. Whatever groups took part came up with an idea. In the church's case, they held an annual rummage and bake sale. Instead of one location, the flyer had a map marking the groups who were taking part in the event. The towns were small, and those involved were only short distances apart. Some locations had games and mazes; others sold fall plants, pumpkins, and decorations; garage sales sprinkled the route. If the weather cooperated, the event was more than a success, and the weather was looking good. The festival would be this weekend. The question from Sara was, did Delia want to come and help set up the rummage sale? They would sort and price clothes, arrange the table for the baked goods, and put up decorations. "How about coming?" Remarkably, Delia said yes. When she hung up, there was a moment of *do I really want to do this?* She tucked that thought away. The exhaustion from the day was winning. The sofa looked very appealing. That's where she landed.

When Sara showed up at the house Friday evening, Delia almost relented, but knew she would never get out of it now and grabbed a jacket as the temperatures were falling.

Twilight was around 6:00 PM, noting that the seasonal change was upon them. The church wasn't far. As they pulled into the driveway, a pleasant building with a large porch overhang was at the forefront. The practical side of Delia was always present. It would give some cover if the weather wasn't good for the sale. The parking lot was reasonably full, and the lights were on. Delia didn't remember the porch addition. They had kept the building well, a necessity in the north country if anything was to last. She took a deep breath. The last time she was here was at her mother's funeral. Delia had enough funerals. Shaking it off, she followed Sara, who introduced (or re-introduced) her to some people. It had been a while and here she was, longer hair and obviously pregnant. The carefree spirit that young girls often showed had long left her. Despite trying to hold herself together while dealing with life, she carried a sadness that was easily sensed. People knew. In small communities, people know.

There was no time for gossip. No one made room for it. There was a ton of stuff, literally. The church made sure the donations were in good shape and strongly emphasized "lightly used" in all their collection campaigns. There were plenty of winter items, household necessities, and toys. With the holiday season in front of everyone, the sale would be popular. There would be a fifty-fifty raffle with the proceeds going to the Care

Fund to help with needs that arise in the congregation. Sara and Delia took half of the bags and set out to separate and price. It was a straightforward assignment. Organizers of the event had given them a suggestion list for pricing specific categories or clothing. There was also enough to keep them busy for at least a couple of hours. Seeing the lay of the land helped Delia to relax. This was the first out of the house and office activity she had been to. The choice was a good one. There were plenty of kids running around; that was at the same time chaotic, but minimally annoying. They were good gophers if you needed anything and just enough of a distraction to keep conversations light and short. People were friendly and inclusive.

After a couple of hours, some women broke out great refreshments, which were welcome and unexpected. Volunteers who finished early helped with cleaning up. Several thanked Delia for coming and said they hoped to see her again tomorrow. That was standard fare for church. It didn't upset her because the comments were genuine and she had fun, at least for a few hours. The constant review of the last months and coming changes that were always running in her head had abated.

She went the next day, surprising even Sara, who asked mechanically about going to the festival and went silent on the phone as Delia responded, "Yes!" The day presented as the perfect Adirondack picture. The fall colors peaked, and the roads and attractions filled with tourists. It was the height of the season. Anyone who was even remotely local knew what would soon chase down this postcard day. Taking advantage of each good moment was a common goal. Today fit the bill.

They got to the church early. Volunteers abounded, as did kids, who were all over and having fun. Some of the older ones monitored tables and helped with coffee, cider, and donuts. You could see they were enjoying the responsibility of overseeing something. They made Delia smile. In return, they waved and offered, "Workers get free coffee and a donut." Sara made a face, implying, "Why not?" With a nod, Delia agreed. She had forgotten how good maple sugar donuts tasted.

There was a steady stream of people that came to the sale, and it was impressive how many found items or gave donations. Conversations were simple and stayed around the weather, local attractions, and upcoming events at the church. It never crossed Delia's mind to be anxious. It was the first time in a long time she was breathing easily while out in a group. They drove home, taking some pumpkins and cupcakes that they had put aside. Both had found items from the sale. Sara helped Delia come up with a few things that could work with her changing shape. An oversized sweater, a pair of slacks with an elastic waistband, mittens, and a matching hat. Sara found a pair of corduroys that had tags on them. The pastor and rummage sale team were serious about the condition of items donated. There were more donations in great shape than you would expect. As they turned down Delia's Street, Sara dove in with, "How about coming to service tomorrow?" She didn't freeze and stiffen as she would normally do but smiled, "I had fun today and last night too, but I'm tired. This was a big weekend for me." Sara nodded. Delia was right. It was a big step, and they had fun. She had pushed enough.

Day 14

The phone rang; it was the hospital. It took a moment for Alina to focus. She had been in a deep sleep. Groggily, she answered.

The charge nurse was calling; it was Delia.

"She woke up disoriented. At first, it sounded as if she knew exactly where she was and what was going on. She was saying she was tired and thirsty. We took that as a significant sign. Then we realized she was back 40 years or more when she was calling for an Anna, saying, don't go? Something about being drafted; you don't have to."

"Anna? Drafted?"

"Yes, doctor. I know that's not her daughter's name. She seemed quite distressed. Dr. Stone ordered a light sedation, and she settled. Her vitals were strong, but you wanted to be informed if anything changed."

"Okay, thanks; I'll come in early. If you gave her something, she should sleep for a while. I need to catch a few more hours too, or I won't be worth much to anyone. If there are any more problems, let me know."

As tired as Alina was, she couldn't help thinking this was different. First, Delia was speaking more than a few short words or syllables. She sounded clear as far as speech but, who was she talking about? That could tell volumes evaluating her clarity and thought process. For 14 days, Delia has been on a silent journey with only a few stirrings that many of her caretakers wondered about. More than once, she walked just under the surface of consciousness. Delia surely had her secrets, but this was a curiosity. Delirium could be a side effect of being intubated. That was a possibility. Alina slipped back to sleep. Young residents learn to catch it when they can.

As promised, she got in early and headed to the small med/surg floor. Overnight, they had an aide, LPN, and one RN who supervised several floors. A doctor was on call. The ER was also open and had a skeleton staff. Nights were problematic. If it hadn't been for this small community hospital and dedicated people, it would be a 45 minute drive to the next nearest one. As she approached the staff's station, they were getting ready to give reports. The next shift would be in shortly. Alina greeted them and found Delia was sleeping with no other changes. Her vitals were good. This was positive news, but didn't solve the puzzle of the night before.

Within the hour, the hospital was bustling as more staff arrived and housekeeping and the kitchen workers started out and about. They had a couple of beds open when they discharged the mother and baby, along with 2 others. This was a solid place to be. The nurse from the local school called. She had seen a growing number of kids she was sending home or whose parents had kept them home because of a stomach like bug. She wanted to give the ER a heads up, as it wouldn't surprise her if some of them came in.

By mid-morning, Alina had finished her rounds and floated in the ER. The school nurse was correct, and they saw some students coming in with a nasty bug requiring fluids. Heading back to the ward, she thought it might be time to check in on Delia.

As Alina entered the room, Delia was sitting up, smiling. Surprised, she greeted her with a simple, "Well, hello! You are looking well!"

"Hello to you, too. It's taken you long enough to get here," was the old woman's response.

That took the young doctor by surprise, and she almost wanted to laugh. Moving closer, Delia startled her by grabbing her hand and drawing her in.

"You look calmer than you were last night. I hope you've come to your senses."

Dr. Levin paused and thought, *where is this going?* She was not sure how to answer, but kept it simple.

"Well, I'm thinking about the pros and cons." That, she thought, was a safe response, not having a clue what the conversation was about.

Delia's expression changed. "The pros and cons? You're kidding. We've been through this, Anna. Please, please!"

She grabbed Alina's arm and again said, "Anna...".

* * *

Fall had been Delia's favorite season. It triggered the approaching holiday preparations and plans. The weather would remain reasonable even through Christmas. There were exceptions, and she had lived them out. Early snowfalls and freezes were not out of the question, but it was a wonderful time of year, until now. She wouldn't even consider the seasonal celebrations; but they were hard to escape with the decorations, festivals, and shops confronting you on every side.

She not only gained weight with her advancing pregnancy, but the emotional heaviness without warning would sweep over her. Grief has stages, she was told. The shifting emotions were not an uncommon accompaniment to pregnancy either. Winters were a challenging season, but now everything felt dark. That was dramatic, yet an accurate description. Sara wore her down; she had periodically started attending church. She had to admit, it helped. The people were friendly, not overbearing. She accepted it was time to get out of the house, as Sara would say, and her father agreed. He wasn't a churchgoer, but seeing his daughter go out and what a good friend she had in Sara comforted him. Those two things raised the church a few notches higher in Tom O'Malley's eyes.

Sara showed up on Sunday, ready to take Delia to church. As always, she could read the signs and asked Delia what was wrong. Delia knew saying nothing was hopeless.

"Mike's parents called and wondered if I'd like to go out to dinner later today. I wanted to say no, but they surprised me, and I couldn't think of a reason to turn them down."

"What's wrong with that? You always liked them, right? That's what you said."

"I know, but it makes me uneasy. I guess I just don't feel comfortable. They've always been supportive. It's silly, but Mike looked so much like his dad. Plus, I don't know how to carry a conversation with them. We've hardly seen each other."

Sara jumped in and said that was the point. They want to be connected. They are the baby's grandparents and you both are all they have left of Mike. She almost regretted saying that and couldn't move on fast enough, as she could see Delia tear up.

"I'm sorry, Delia. I shouldn't have said that."

"It's not you. Of course, you're right. They were always warm and supportive. They would never be a problem, which is why I said I would go."

Sara simply said it was good and thought it would turn out fine. Delia had no response. The conversation moved on. Church was as expected. Delia was sure it was more than that, but she was so distracted and becoming more uncomfortable sitting for longer periods of time.

It wasn't the healthiest, but after service, they got some pie and coffee at the local diner. Tourists were enjoying late breakfasts or brunch, whatever they called it. Sara was good at small talk and kept chattering. She asked if Delia would like to go to the movies in Saranac sometime. When she saw the hesitancy, she reminded her they could go to a Saturday matinee and catch dinner out. Delia remembered she and Mike had gone to the movies a few times and walked around Saranac looking in shops and taking in the people. That was an inexpensive but a little different date than staying in town. Emotions were creeping in. They headed home, so she'd have time to do a few things and maybe rest before the Parkers came to pick her up.

Sara dropped her off and said she needed to relax.

"Call me later and let me know how it went. I'm sure you'll be fine."

Delia was grateful for her friend. Sara had a grounding effect. Saying she'd be there made a big difference. It offered a connection to someone who understood there was an endless mixture of emotions to walk out. Delia didn't have to explain anything but could if she wanted to. That meant everything. She loved her family and knew there was affection for the Parkers, but it wasn't like she could talk to them or explain how she felt or what was bothering her.

They arrived on time. The Parkers stood there a little anxious when Delia opened the door; they were smiling. She quietly stepped back and moved her hand to come in. A moment of hesitation led to a hug by Mike's mother, who was on the verge of tears. It had been three months since they had seen Delia and now the reality of a grandchild was more than clear. She hugged her daughter-in-law, leaving Delia's fears to slip away.

The visit was cheerful. Not at all what she was expecting, but happy with the outcome. Even when they talked about Mike, it wasn't as painful as it could be and more about what he was like and how the baby might be. They stayed local for dinner rather than taking the time driving. Mike's mom said she was crocheting a blanket for the baby and had picked up a few things. By the end of dinner, they headed over to the park for a walk. The approaching sunset and fall foliage were amazing and put the perfect ending to the visit. When the Parkers left, Delia didn't feel the relief she thought. It was a warmth and a connection to Mike. That was the last thing she had expected.

For at least a while, there was comfort and even hope. There wasn't any part of the pregnancy that she enjoyed and now that was changing. She was going to call Sara, but not just yet savoring the visit. The family settled into their routine: Sunday night TV, *The Ed Sullivan Show, and Mission Impossible.* Mission Impossible, that was relatable. Some say sarcasm is good. That it's a sign of humor brought to difficult situations; you're a survivor. Maybe she was improving; life was improving. It didn't feel as heavy as it had been over the last few months.

It was a good weekend and hoped for more. She felt guilty even thinking that way with all the days she had missed. The nausea subsided, but her appetite changed. She ate because she had to, not because she enjoyed food or because it tasted good. Others often reminded her she was eating for two. She smiled, thinking, *remember that with ice cream or pie.* A steady work situation with flex hours; Sara's friendship, reconnecting with Mike's parents, even church and getting out, all made a difference.

Day 15

The interaction with Delia had quickly slipped from excitement to concern. The old woman spoke coherently, even fluently, at the start of the conversation. Everything was so normal; then she quickly appeared delusional, determined that Alina was someone else, Anna. Not only was Delia convinced that she was this other person, but there was also anger that brought out a different demeanor. This from the sick and weak woman who had teetered on the brink of life for the last two weeks.

Alina did her best to remain calm with Delia, who was agitated, saying that she would think about things as she held the old woman's hands. Peace returned. There was no blackout or any other extraneous behaviors. It was over, just like that. During the outburst, Alina met Delia's eyes, and she focused with a steely expression. It was disturbing. The young doctor reported to the nurses what had occurred and asked them to monitor her closely, noting anything abnormal. Nothing in her vitals changed. She had gotten excited, but thankfully, it didn't trigger anything else. Whatever it was, had passed; a peace returned.

There were more patients and fewer doctors. With no life-threatening situation, it was time to move on. Limited staff called for efficiency for whatever team was up. Though she had more patients, none were critical; some were quite sick, but no threatening emergencies on the horizon, at least not in the hospital and not now. Alina knew this was a fragile peace during these unique times. Something was in the air. Several weather forecasts were calling for a drop in temperature, maybe into the 40s overnight. It was fall, but that wasn't an accurate barometer in the Adirondacks. Change was coming and elicited another avenue for media response. They painted the dreaded picture of what summer's end could mean. Every weather forecast with a hint of a storm was an 'event'. Schools were opening and cooler temps were driving people indoors and threatening the spread of the virus. The bad news was always there.

Alina was still hopeful. Compared to the previous week, things were moving at a steady, manageable pace. There was a bed crunch, but with a little juggling and creative thinking, they could usually work through it, at least so far. The influx of tourists could change that instantly. Alina was learning to live more in the moment, one battle at a time. It was stressful to let yourself go beyond that. Nothing was following any previous pattern: the idea of a lockdown, masks, rules, testing for admittance to varying situations, airports and travel limitations. The expansive reach of the virus frazzled the steadiness of the most stalwart. Who would think masking and vaccines would fuel bitter arguments and divisions, even amongst families? Family. This had been a strange day, and it made Alina decide she wanted to call her grandparents. She would do that later. They had been in touch with email, letters, and phone calls. She was close to her grandparents and loved and appreciated them. Today, the encounter with Delia felt personal. Alina couldn't figure why that would be. Yes, she invested in this woman, but for her, that was what you did for a patient. Why should this be different now?

After work, a quick stop home to get Jax, and then off to the park. It was a balmy day. A slight breeze followed her and her four-legged partner. The park was busy, but not crowded. She was familiar with the trails now and chose a longer one with some minor climbs; it was also one that followed the lake. The sky was clear. This was a perfect answer to stress. By the time she finished the trail, she felt better. Alina found the outdoors activated a response, as an antidote for what ailed her. After they got home, she felt like cooking and grilled some steak. Her grandmother taught her some basics so she could whip up cheesy biscuits without thinking about it. By early evening, she revived and dialed home.

Her grandmother picked up the phone, and she could hear the excitement in her voice. The conversation was easy. How are you doing? Tell me about your friends? What's the weather like there? We miss you. So it went. Alina and her grandmother talked for about a half hour. She felt she couldn't hang up. It was lingering; she knew it had driven the decision to call. Her stomach was in knots.

"Grandma, is there anyone in our family named Anna?"

* * *

As Delia headed through the door, fellow workers offered a few quick greetings. The office was a well-oiled machine where order prevailed. People could think that would be boring, but it was comforting. She was relaxing and that sense of being overwhelmed was dropping off. Life was far from perfect, but dread when her eyes opened in the morning occurred less frequently. She wasn't missing any more work. That was a help and relief too. For a while, it seemed she couldn't get out of constantly having to worry about everything. Nothing is more energy consuming than worry. The worst part, it produces nothing. *When will we humans learn that?*

"Delia," turning she met Mr. Wells' smile.

He greeted her amiably and asked her to stop by his office around 10:00. She nodded and said, "Of course," and wondered what it might be about. Curiosity caught her off guard; yet he was smiling and seemed positive. It was a long hour, but she had plenty to do at her desk. The company was busy, especially with some of the new projects he had started.

10:00 o'clock came. Mr. Wells' office had clear windows, and Delia could see him busy at his desk. The door was open, and she knocked lightly. With a quick smile, he greeted her and waved her in. There was small talk about how she was feeling, compliments on the quality of her work, and then a surprise. She listened as Mr. Wells explained how the temporary employment service he had been working on was picking up. Then he asked her the question.

"Delia, there's a lot of paperwork involved with an employment service. The need has grown beyond what I had imagined. We are servicing multiple companies and job seekers whom I have handled up to this point, but I'm bringing Ella in to oversee this service. She will need help. Would you be interested in joining her? It would involve helping job applicants fill out initial paperwork; then you would match their skills with the companies we're servicing. It would be a modest raise. You would do the filing and phones you are currently doing. The raise would reflect the extra responsibilities and its ebbs and flows. Some days will be busy and others slower. Once you know what the job seekers need to do, it should not take too much extra time. Ella will deal with the companies and interview potential candidates."

It took her aback, and she tried to process it all at the same time. It was a promotion and some extra money. How could she pass that up?

"What do you think?"

"Yes, I'm interested. What about when the baby comes?"

"I think we can work it out. Right now, you will help Ella. Between the two of you, I'm sure you'll develop a system to organize this. The flex hours are something I am keeping in place. That should help too. We'll work it out."

He ended with a warm smile that encouraged her to eke out a weak, "Yes!" A thank you followed.

Mr. Wells had to be one of the kindest men she'd ever met. The people in the office were also a tremendous support. She struggled with the idea of not deserving it, but her father quickly squelched that when he heard the news.

"Of course you deserve it. You're a steady, hardworking employee and you're smart!"

That evoked a laugh from Delia and her brothers, who were also present. It felt good to laugh. She couldn't remember the last time.

When Sara called that night, Delia was excited to have some good news to share. Her friend agreed. There was nothing to feel guilty about. "Go for it, girl. It's the first time I've seen you look forward to something. I think it's great."

It appeared to be settled. Sara had called to extend another invitation. This time, the church was having a potluck supper. She related they had them frequently at one time, but it seemed to have fallen off. The next question had her laughing again.

"Can you cook?"

"Good enough," was Delia's response plus a query with what do you need? They decided that homemade macaroni and cheese and corn bread would be perfect. No matter what, it would be a hit with the kids for sure and could be a side dish to multiple other items Sara knew were already on the menu. They settled it. Anything to keep her friend involved. She also knew the family would need help when the baby came. Connections matter. That's where she was coming from but could see, happily, that Delia was breaking out of the sadness that had gripped her life. Everyone needs a friend who sees what's at stake and stays with you for the long run. Sara was that friend. The rest of the week was uneventful. Delia had picked up the groceries needed for her Sunday outing, making sure she included enough for her father and brothers at home. It didn't go unnoticed by them either. She seemed lighter.

It was early November, and fall was evident at every turn. The days were shorter and the trees almost bare, telling of the coming winter. Delia was also changing. Her slender body was filling out more noticeably now, as she was in her second trimester. Life had settled into a steady pace. There wasn't a day that went by when she didn't think about Mike. Her heart ached, and she missed him; but it wasn't the deep depression from the beginning. She had conversations in her head with him; nothing weird or mystical; he wasn't talking back. She imagined what she would say about the baby who was growing, about work, Sara, and life. Nothing was too small, even the weather. It brought a closeness; she felt Mike wouldn't mind. The Parkers kept in touch and tried to make it a habit to have dinner every month with Delia and her family. It seems these were the best outcomes for the great loss that had affected all of them. Second trimester. Everyone described that as the best time during a pregnancy. The nausea passed and the heaviness of the third trimester and increased discomforts were not with her yet.

Fall and early winter had always been her favorite times. No extreme weather was threatening, and the holiday season would soon be upon them. Grieving a loss during the holidays can pose serious problems; the baby was tempering the loss somewhat. Oh, if she could change things! She missed Mike more than she could speak, but had to keep going. Sometimes she felt guilty even thinking that, and could hear her father's voice about how insane it was. *Feeling guilty? What did she have to feel guilty about?* A smile would appear on her face. He was her biggest cheerleader, and she knew he was processing all the changes the family was going through, too. A soon to be grandfather was one of them.

A crowd packed the church on Sunday. Food was always a good draw, and everyone accepted the fact some of the best cooks were found during potluck meals. Delia wasn't used to the crowds. Until now, she felt she could get lost in them and practiced that, a philosophy which didn't hold up at church. People were forever introducing themselves and questions followed. She knew they meant well, and the questions were innocent.

Some new families had joined the congregation during the last few months, the Hansons, the Millers and the Browns. Throughout the afternoon, Sara introduced her to them. With their children, they added almost twenty people to the church. The three families jumped right in and were ready to help. With the holidays coming, there would be more activities, festivals, and services. Each season brought its own special events, and the church would welcome more volunteers. Amongst their children were a range of ages, from toddler to adult. They had even brought businesses to the community. The Hansons were excavators and took over the sand and gravel business outside of town. The Millers had family in the area who owned the general store, and the Browns were contractors. All were solid additions to the community. Good or bad, there was a small exodus from the cities. People wanted their own businesses and a different lifestyle; the Adirondacks were a perfect setting for them.

Day 16

The phone call ended fine. Her grandmother couldn't recall an Anna in the family. Alina knew it was probably a longshot, but she couldn't shake whatever she was feeling about this woman she had been caring for. It was especially unnerving how Delia looked at her, but obviously it was a coincidence. Alina reminded Delia of someone; she wasn't off meds or totally lucid. It was an understandable mistake.

That night was the first decent sleep she'd had in quite a while. She was heading to work, feeling prepared. Gabe was returning as well. Alina hoped he had rested and regained his strength. Covid was far-reaching and sapped energy that people fought to regain. She hoped it wouldn't be that way for Gabe.

So far, the Adirondacks weren't a disappointment with their beauty or the weather. Alina smiled, remembering. She hadn't been through a winter yet. Savoring the moment was the best plan. The ER was busy, but under control. Added to the typical stomach bugs and colds, they were seeing allergies, respiratory infections, and poison ivy. Injuries from work projects, gardening and roughhouse play were also on the list of complaints. This was what Alina had hoped for. It provided a range of experiences from the pressure and early days of the pandemic to the seasonal issues, the regular cases that most ERs will see. She kept that in mind and was grateful when any peaceful days came. Without going too far, she heard a familiar voice.

"Well, it's about time you came in!"

"Me? Says the one who's been milking days off."

"You got me," said Gabe with a smile.

He knew she had been working flex hours, trying to fill in where needed. Within moments, both were called to arms and the day's battles began. By midafternoon, the temperatures were rising into the high 70s, a little unusual but not out of the question for early fall. That didn't faze Alina, who was from the south, but the northerners didn't relish such heat. The news was calling for successive temps in that range which designated it as a heatwave. The day ambled on and at shift's end, Gabe caught up with Alina.

"Hey, got any plans?"

"You talkin to me," Alina replied, laughing.

"How about some takeout and fishing?"

"You have a boat?"

"I do! It's at the launch. I'll bring Eddie, and you can bring Jax. What do you think?"

Alina had smiled and tilted her head, asking,

"Is this a date?"

"And what if it is?"

She took a moment and said, "Okay."

A simple and clear response. Gabe filled in the details. He would go home, order something, change, and get Eddie. They would pick her up in about an hour. Alina smiled and said she and Jax would be ready. Cami was standing close, and the exchange didn't go unnoticed. Alina turned and caught her eye with an expression that beckoned, "What?" The nurse shook her head and responded with her eyes. Nothing escaped her, which most of the time was her best quality. Alina headed out the doors and to her car. It was warm for fall. She looked forward to being on the water. It would be peaceful, and Gabe was easy to be with.

He was on time and had grabbed deli sandwiches, drinks, and cheeses. Alina had brownies she had put together the day before.

"It looks like we're ready for a long ride. At least we won't go hungry."

"I like to be prepared," Gabe responded with a wry smile.

"Prepared for what?"

"Oh, I don't know. I was a boy scout; that's how they trained us."

Alina laughed and felt relieved of the newness of the situation.

"Where are we going?"

Gabe responded they were heading out of town toward Harrison's Landing, where Anne Ward's clinic was. Just before town, there was a turnoff that would take them to Spitfire Lake. She thought that was a strange name, and it surprised her they weren't going to the park in town. Gabe explained the lake was private, with no public access. He had friends that let him use their launch area. One was an old woodsman named Noah Johnson and the other a professor from Paul Smith's, Caitlin Morrisey.

"The lake is beautiful, and the surrounding mountains are outstanding. A crisscross of country roads weaves throughout. If we get lucky, maybe we'll see some wildlife; deer for sure, and maybe a bear."

"Bear?"

"No worries. There's plenty of food for them this time of year. You wouldn't be of interest."

Her expression was enough to keep him laughing. They pulled off the road onto another rougher road that led down to the lake. It was a beautiful and quiet spot. Someone had taken time to carve out an area with an exquisite view. Adirondack chairs with a small table and a fire pit were close to the shoreline, but on a little incline. A hundred feet or more off to one side was a boat launch. There was a small but respectable boat that made it easy enough for Gabe to maneuver. He parked the car and suggested getting what they would need to get a fire going later.

He impressed her. Effort had gone into this evening; it was genuine and welcomed. The air was refreshing by the water; the temperature wasn't much different from town, but there was a slight breeze and an enveloping quiet.

Gabe could see she was thinking. "What's on your mind?"

"Mostly nothing. It's so quiet and beautiful here. There's a tranquility."

"And?"

"And? Doctor Stewart, very perceptive of you."

"Not so much. I think anyone could see something was on your mind. I was hoping, maybe me?"

Alina laughed out loud and splashed some water on him. He didn't let her off that easily.

"The older woman with Covid that you have weaned off the ventilator."

She nodded and said, "Yeah, that's Delia. She's making slow progress; any progress is good. One reason I came north is I wanted a fresh setting. This is different. I also wanted a smaller hospital where I could spend more time with my patients. I worked in the ER in a very large urban hospital. It felt like people were on a conveyor belt. I was excited to come here."

"Are you disappointed?"

"No, no... quite the opposite. I love having more time with patients and colleagues. Delia is an enigma. It's approaching 2 ½ weeks, and she's not totally well enough to go home. There are moments when she's awake but not lucid. I guess what's bothered me is she thinks I'm someone else. She grabbed my hand and looked at me with a strange expression. A couple of days ago, she sounded perfectly normal, but then got angry with me and called me Anna. She was angry with this Anna."

"Have you spoken with her family?"

"I usually talk with her daughter, Karen. She wasn't available when I called and yesterday and today, we were busy."

Gabe looked, "What else?"

"You're pushy!"

"Again, what else?"

This took her aback. She paused, even surprising herself. There was another reason.

"My mom was from the Adirondacks. I don't know much. No one does. My father's parents raised me because my mother and he were in the Army. She died in Afghanistan.

There's an entire piece of my life missing." There was a pause and Gabe spoke up.

"Do something about it!"

* * *

The office transitions were smooth. Delia started working with Ella, and the two became good friends. She liked the change and enjoyed meeting candidates who were looking for employment. They were eager for her help with their applications; she was glad to be helpful and not on the spot to do the hiring. Ella could organize and was the perfect fit for managing the employment service. She had confidence engaging businesses who were looking for employees. Ella had the experience and handled interviews well, business-like but relatable. As a friend, she differed from Sara, older, maybe in her 30s and single, and was easy to talk to, a genuinely nice person.

The weather was shifting with cooler temperatures appearing more frequently. Delia's slender figure was changing with each passing day. She told Sara it was time to get some maternity clothes. There was a store, Second Time Around, that had gently used clothing and other home items. Someone from church mentioned there was a small section for maternity clothing and assured her the clothes were good, truly gently used. She wanted a coat of some sort and maybe a jumper or slacks. The woman also said that she was small enough to try a larger size, especially with a jumper. These were good ideas and with the weekend coming, it was on the list to check out.

Life continued as it does. Additional responsibilities contributed to work becoming more enjoyable. Delia found she liked working with applicants. Getting to know people's skills and goals was interesting. She was more relaxed than she originally thought she'd be. The days no longer dragged on. With the seasonal changes and holidays approaching, there was an expectation. Delia knew Mike would never want her to remain grieving. That's not who he was. When she felt guilty, her response was to get busy doing something. That was easier than thinking about it.

The days were shorter, and snow was in the air. At the beginning of winter, it was a novelty. Once December passed, she knew things would change. Storms would bring some trying times with bad roads and power outages. These were not news to anyone who lived in the area. Thanksgiving was approaching. Although it had been the most trying year of her life, there had been enjoyable moments. She tried to focus there. For her, this was progress. The family planned to have the holiday at the O'Malley's. Aunt Janie would come with her daughter, and they would bring the turkey. Her father invited an old bachelor friend from work, Ed Gillis, who was like an uncle to them. He would bring some of his special bread; he loved to bake, probably some spirits too. Delia smiled and thought, *A good plan!* Those elements were the center of the meal, and no one wanted a fail there. They could survive the rest, and she was improving in her culinary skills so she would tackle dessert. At church, they were planning a community meal to make sure everyone had the opportunity for a solid Thanksgiving dinner. This was the Sunday before the holiday. Everyone knew the Christmas season followed with the culmination of turkey day.

Delia knew of another event that was looming. Sara organized a baby shower. She had seen an invitation mistakenly left out on Sara's desk at work, but wasn't going to snoop any further. The who and when on the guest list were unclear. It had always been hard for Delia to accept gifts or anything that put the spotlight on her; that hadn't changed and, in some ways, increased in this recent period. She didn't want to worry about it and did her best not to think of the impending event, knowing it was inevitable. Realistically, they weren't prepared for a baby at home. It would be helpful. The Parkers had picked up a few things here and there. They knew the baby was a girl. Delia hadn't said much about it. Somehow, knowing it was a girl made things more real. For just a moment, she thought about a name, but quickly dismissed the thought. Her due date was in early March. That was something else she didn't talk about.

Life had settled down. She was trying hard to savor the moments that weren't chaotic; work, for example, was settling into a new but pleasant rhythm. It was also a place where her boss and co-workers were supportive of her and the baby and kept reassuring her it would all work out. Delia had barely accepted the assurance. Life doesn't work that way. We are rarely ready for most things. Andy Brown was another surprise.

The Browns had moved to Hillstown in early summer. His father and brothers were contractors, as he was, truly a family business. The suburbs just north of New York suffered from an exodus. The economy and socio-political atmosphere entreated new horizons and entrepreneurs. People could agree on little except the fact that changes were in the air. It was not uncommon to hear conversations about *getting the kids out of the city.* That was the case with the Browns. The family was almost 2 families, the younger Browns and the older 3 sons. Two of the sons were drafted. One had returned home with an injury; another remained overseas. Andy wasn't either. He had asthma. Hard to imagine, but some considered it lucky as it kept him from Viet Nam. He was an excellent business manager and had a quick mind for most things related to construction and finances. Beyond that, there was a ready smile and a kind spirit. The two younger children were 8 and 10. The Browns were generous and had strong family values and faith.

It didn't take long for them to assimilate into the church, and the process was genuine. They not only attended, but jumped in and served wherever needed. Within a short period, they were known and liked in the community and surrounding townships.

The day before the Thanksgiving Dinner at church, volunteers set up the dining hall for the meal that would follow the Sunday service. Delia had grown to enjoy these events. If it hadn't been for Sara...

"Well, here she is!"

"I sense some tone in that comment," replied Sara.

Delia laughed and said nothing. She was thinking about the first time she came and helped. A voice interrupted.

"Hello ladies! I was told to grab another couple of tables for drinks and desserts. Where do you want them?" Sara spoke up. She pointed along the wall to the left and asked Delia to get the tablecloths and napkins; she would look for the coffee makers and drink dispensers. When she got back to the tables, Andy had just finished securing the second one. He turned to her and caught her off guard, saying, "Delia, right?" She didn't know what to do. How silly that seemed when only a simple greeting was required, which she finally got out.

"Here, I'll help with the tablecloths."

She wasn't responding and thought *there's something wrong with me.* Andy was unphased and didn't miss a beat. It's hard to keep a conversation going when the other person says nothing, but Sara returned just in time. You could count on her to assess a situation and save it.

"I'll get the tableware, and we can wrap it in the napkins. I always thought that was silly, but it helps to keep the line moving."

Andy asked, "About how many settings do we need?"

Delia said she didn't know, and that she wasn't here last Thanksgiving. His reply was quick that they were both newbies.

"Newbies?"

"Right, both of us haven't been around or part of the congregation for a long time. Where are you from?"

Delia felt a little put off talking to this young man, but he was affable and persistent. It crossed her mind that not too many men his age would even talk to a woman in her condition.

"Oh, I'm from around here, Hillstown. I have only been coming to the church for a little while. Sara invited me. We work together. I came here years ago as a child and stopped when my mother died. She was the one who kept us coming."

"I know how that works. Family dynamics change. Life happens. My older brothers went to Viet Nam; one came back wounded. The other is still there. The politics of this country are tense. That's how my parents came to move upstate. They felt it was better to raise the family in a more rural setting. I have a younger brother and sister."

It made sense, hearing the same sentiments in her own family. This was a beautiful area and a friendly community. Some would think perfect for raising a family. Sara, again, interrupted the conversation, and not a minute too soon. Delia didn't want to think about raising a family. As nice as Andy was, she couldn't take the conversation any longer. Sara's radar could read her friend and discreetly asked for help in the kitchen. Delia was relieved. Andy was pleasant and helpful, but she felt out of place, even nervous. He annoyed her, just when things seemed to be comfortable.

"So, what was that about?" Now Sara's quip got to her.

"What are you talking about?"

"Please, you were giving me the eye; you wanted to be rescued."

"Really? Can't imagine that a pregnant widow wouldn't want to play cute? Get serious. He started talking about how this was a good place to raise a family. Can't you understand how I would feel?"

"I can, but you will have to face things like this. You're only 18 years old. As hard as it is, life will go on. I'm sorry and don't mean to sound callous."

"I know and no one means any harm but a six months pregnant, 18-year-old widow. It's awkward. I feel like talking to him is wrong."

"It's simple talk at a church workday. The family is new in town. That's it. You can't hide away and not talk to people."

"That he's a young 20ish male makes it different." Delia's expression was a mix of emotions, from anxiety to firmness.

Sara understood. "Okay, this conversation needs a change. They need you in the kitchen and wondered about making pumpkin pie pudding? They think the younger kids might like it instead of pie."

Delia smiled. It was time to move the moment on. She enjoyed being called in on a cooking or bakery task. That she could handle and was grateful. It took more than another hour to make a few batches of the pudding, which had turned out quite good. She was tired. Sara had been all over doing a variety of different assignments. By now, the sun said it was late afternoon, and so did her legs. Delia thought, *enough!* Tomorrow would be busier yet. Right now, she didn't feel up to it, but knew a little rest would set things right.

"Okay, I saw the look," said Sara.

"Yeah, I'm ready. It's been good, and the pudding turned out great."

Day 17

Alina contemplated the evening. It had been relaxing, yet interesting enough to raise questions. She wasn't ready to think about that now. Sleep, that's what she wanted. She had air conditioning, but the evening cooled, and the open windows were her first choice. The summer was passing and in spots here and there, fall was in the air. It was always so quiet on her street, especially later in the evening, a perfect answer to insure a good night's sleep. On the busiest days, when her mind had raced from one patient or problem to another, she found solace in the comforting setting of her little cottage apartment. Sleep came within moments of hitting the pillow.

She awoke with a jolt and looked at her phone; She felt relieved. The alarm hadn't gone off, but her sleep was so deep it was startling. You wake up and wonder where you are and what did you miss? That sent her mind spiraling back to Delia, the lake with Gabe, and questions about the day ahead. Coffee. That would bring her into the day's agenda and get her moving.

She had a cup at home and picked up one on the way to work. Today, she picked up a Box O' Joe for the staff too, and why not? Donut holes, too, which were perfect on the run.

Alina put the coffee down at the nurse's station.

Cami was right there with a quick comment.

"Must have been a good evening. Dr. Stewart came in whistling and now you come bearing gifts."

Two others smirked, and Alina could feel her face flush. She brushed it off and worked through her messages and the overnight report. It was all she could think of and didn't want to process any comments. Besides, she had nothing to say. It was a date. That's all. Right?

They were almost full as far as beds. There was a slight lull with the virus, but no one was ready to let their guard down. A few minor surgeries; a couple of cases of pneumonia, one a child and more covid cases. The notes on Delia showed nothing extraordinary. It appeared Delia had a good night. Alina walked into her room and the old woman greeted her with a flat, "Hello, Dr. Levin." Interesting. Though Delia was clearer than she had appeared on Alina's last shift, the greeting was lifeless. There was no apparent struggle, but a somewhat depressed delivery. The good part was that she knew who Alina was. No confusion. The young doctor went forward with a series of simple questions; how was she feeling? Any pain issues, nausea; she followed with questions about family, where she was and so on. The physical side was also acceptable, with some expected weakness after being in bed for so long. Alina kept the conversation moving and noted maybe it was time to get in the chair and sit by the window, hoping that would lead to short walks. All of this to prepare for a discharge. It was time to see if that's where they were really heading.

A nurse came in and together they helped Delia sit with her legs on the side of the bed. So far, it seemed good.

"I don't think I can do this today."

"It's okay, Delia; sitting is fine. We don't have to do anything. You have been in bed for a while now. It's important to take it slow."

The situation was perplexing. As slow and difficult as this had been, Alina would have to say there was progress. She would take it. Tomorrow was another day.

When she finished the morning rounds, there would be a few discharges, which was good for the patients and the hospital. She got the paperwork in order. Anne Riley Ward was coming in. Doctors Keeler and Stone were off. Word had it that Anne was looking for a doctor to partner in the town clinic in Harrison's Landing. Alina knew that was good for the locals; she couldn't quite figure the hospital's place in the trajectory. Primary health care is important. When individuals have primary providers, it's usually the right way to go and hospitals can benefit. It was undeniable that losing another hospital physician or staffer would be very difficult. No one could even project the future. Who would have imagined a world pandemic and any of the outcomes? Life was day to day because openings, closings, vaccines, shortages, and more were a daily sea of waves to navigate. Who could imagine anything? Along with a seemingly endless dissemination of misinformation, truth was a constant quest. No matter how transparent you would try to be, someone always had an issue. It was exhausting.

Late summer days were delightful, and trips to the lake became routine. Despite the craziness of the world, Alina was happy. There were hints of fall. Cooler nights and isolated trees brought traces of kaleidoscopic color. Some people love the four seasons and would speak of enjoying the changes they always bring. Whatever the hardships, those who welcomed them found something for which they could be grateful. The seasons called out an anticipation, even if it didn't persist. There was an expectation of something new. She felt that, maybe not just about the seasons....

* * *

Church was packed and the fellowship hall not only was festive but full of food; it all looked wonderful. When service was over, there were a few announcements. Volunteers headed to their stations to help the dinner lines move more smoothly. Delia heard a voice and turned. She was at the drink table. It was Andy Brown. Immediate thoughts of dread ran through her head. They must have been on her face. He responded, "I wanted to say I'm sorry about yesterday. I came on strong and sort of invaded your space. I just wanted to be friendly and didn't mean to make you uncomfortable. Being new to the area is difficult, especially at my age. It's not like going to school and making new friends instantly. I'm working for my father, part of his business. I have no complaints, but it makes having a social life difficult. So, friends, okay?"

She had been fussing through the entire speech. The table didn't need fussing. Andy's affable way reduced her initial stress. Unsure, but wanting to get past the moment, she extended her hand and quietly said, "Friends."

The holiday season began. The sense of community was strong and hopeful. Again, moments that took Delia by surprise. It was another long day. Her dad and brothers came as they had promised and, honestly, she thought they had a good time. Certainly, there were no complaints about the food and the church made take home bags for leftovers. The men in the O'Malley family were ever ready. She also noted her brothers talking to the Brown brothers. Not surprising, as Andy said, it was hard to make friends, and he and her brothers were probably about the same age.

The crowd dwindled, and only a few of the volunteers remained. Delia had to sit down. When Sara noticed her, she could see how tired she was and felt it was thoughtless that she didn't notice sooner.

"Ready to go?"

Delia nodded. She didn't answer. That worried Sara. "You sure?"

"Yes, I'll be fine. I just need to get off my feet. It was a great dinner. Everyone had a good time."

With a wry smile, Sara asked, "You too?"

Delia's answer was simple, "Yeah, me too."

Day 18

The weekend had been busy, probably too busy for Delia. She was determined to get to work. Once she made it through the first trimester, and all the events that had occurred, she hadn't missed a day's work. Mr. Wells had been so kind, she was determined to repay his kindness by being the most dedicated and hard-working employee. Delia hadn't missed any more days and wanted to keep it that way as long as possible. She knew Mr. Wells and Ella would work out a plan when the baby was born. The goal was no more time off.

With determination, she got up and started the day's routine. A quick shower, then downstairs for coffee and breakfast. Her father was always the first up. Sometimes his need to talk was a bit much, but his coffee was more than welcome today. He saw the exhaustion and, amazingly, said nothing. She was grateful. The shower and food helped, especially the coffee. The week had begun.

Once you get to work, it all falls into place, and it's almost as if the weekend didn't happen. Life goes on. How true that expression had become for Delia. Life went on without Mike. A few short months, a new position at work, a baby on the way, new friends, and church. Too much to think about. At that moment, a job seeker came in and Delia stepped up to help. She found even her interactions with people had changed, developed more. A confidence grows with challenges met. Whether the assurance was genuine or forced, it suited her. Only a few weeks had passed since the expanded program was under way, and Mr. Wells complemented Ella and Delia for how well the employment service was running. He could see their initial endeavor would need to expand. They had gained several businesses, including the hospital, all who were eager to fill positions. Wells had wondered if the service would be viable; ironically, because of the area's unique profile, workers of all types were in demand for seasonal and year round work. The agency flourished and, with the holidays getting underway, those seasonal workers were in even greater demand.

Winter arrived shortly after Thanksgiving. There was something peaceful about the first snow. That always sounded so romanticized. It quickly wore off. Dark days and cold temps wear on the nerves of most people during the long upstate winters. The Christmas season helps many to hold on to a more hopeful outlook for a little while. That would be difficult for Delia this year, even with all the positive additions to her life. She had always thought about having her own home and how the holidays would be with her husband and children. It was a very Currier and Ives view. Culturally, it would portray the perfect home that fits well, especially in rural communities.

She was starting her seventh month, the beginning of her third trimester. Time is such a mystery, feeling as if it's been forever since she first found out she was pregnant. Now, struggling to put into reality, she would have a baby before too long, a matter of weeks. It became so with the shower. It was at Aunt Janie's house. She insisted. Delia felt comfortable with the familiar surroundings, and it was only a few blocks away. That would help with getting the gifts home afterwards. Practicality remained one of Delia's best traits. There were decorations, pink of course. Lots of food and a beautiful cake waited on the table. A reasonable but not overwhelming group of women were actively chatting. Aunt Janie planned some games and Sara went along with them. Diaper changing relays and word scrambles tested more than skills. Delia didn't want to, but went through with it and was relieved when they were over. The gifts varied, and were generous and needed, from diapers to a changing table and a group gift of a crib. Delia was very grateful. The conversations were simple but tiring. She didn't really want to talk much, but that was hard when the shower was for you.

"Delia."

When she heard her name, she turned. It was Sara's mom.

"Have you decided on a name yet?"

She had been thinking and was struggling... another step she didn't want to take. It would bring everything closer. Though it was only a second or so that she drifted, suddenly she could see that Sara's mom was waiting for that answer.

"I was thinking of Annaliese. It was a name I've always liked. If not for a first name, maybe a middle name."

And so it was. Mary Catherine Annaliese Parker was born on March 15th. It wasn't easy. Birthing a child never is, but Delia had done well. Her father and the Parkers were beyond thrilled with their granddaughter. Mary Catherine was Mike's grandmother's name and Annaliese was a name the young couple just liked. Not that they had time to plan; it was just one of those layered conversations that came up when they were dating under the 'what ifs' or 'what names do you like?' They would laugh and move on quickly; most couples have those conversations long before anything is firm. It's like testing the waters. Delia's brothers were all over being uncles and bought some interesting toys which she wouldn't use for a few years. It made Delia laugh, and for a moment, the other feelings subsided. She wondered, *What would Mike be doing now? How would he feel?* Those thoughts passed and weren't profitable, not that she would forget. Reality had risen above anything else. She was a mother and had a new life. That was the reality. Company came with food and more gifts. The generosity of everyone overwhelmed her. Family, old friends, people from church. It had been a week now since Anna was born. She would call her that, but Mary Catherine stuck with the family. Not only was it her given name, but her grandfather was an O'Malley and an Irishman who beamed with pride for little Mary Catherine. That was okay with Delia. Everyone had enough sorrow.

Winter was long as usual. The months never change, but patience grows short, and people become anxious for better weather and more sunshine. It had been almost 7 months since the news of Mike's death. They had been the most tumultuous months of her life. Moments of peace came more often now. When she looked into her baby's face, there was a joy that rose within. Her eyes were Mike's and with that came a closeness that she had missed. To her, this was Anna. The name they would have chosen together.

By April, the sun came more often, and warmer temperatures teased of days ahead. Work was great; some days she went in later. Appointments with clients were flexible and worked for her. She brought the baby with her when appointments were at odd hours. She and Ella worked out the schedule. Aunt Janie helped when schedule changes were unavoidable. Mr. Wells was almost like a grandfather. Anna had a wide and loving circle.

It continued to grow. Andy Brown had become a good friend. He kept his word and respected her space. She found him easy to talk to and funny. He was talented at helping with the baby as well. As always, Sara remained her best friend, one who had walked her out of her darkest times into the light. She remembered how she resisted Sara's promptings, even resented them. Despite her moodiness, Sara never succumbed to her dark side. Delia was very grateful for that. There were moments, but life was changing.

Moving forward! That sounded so trite, as if anyone could just move forward from the loss of a husband. Time doesn't really heal, but it presses on. What she couldn't deny is the fact she enjoyed Andy Brown's company. At first, there was resistance. It wasn't until almost a year after Mike had died that she even allowed herself to really talk to him. A guilt arose any time someone teasingly brought him up. Again, he was faithful not to press her and was helpful, cheerful, and decent. He was older, certainly not old, late twenties. His family had a strong business as contractors. They did excellent work in a timely way. It had to be said, they were affable, easy people to be around. She remembered how church was almost their first stop and they were ready and willing volunteers. That says something. It was close to two years since they had moved to Hilltown, and these qualities remained true.

It wasn't as it had been with Mike. Andy was uncomplicated and a friendship. Comfortable. Some would consider that not a complimentary way to describe a person, but Delia thought it was perfect. The truth—she didn't think. That's what made it the best. She enjoyed working together at church. They even sat together since her family didn't attend. When Sara wasn't available, he picked her up and drove them to church, especially when the weather wasn't good. These came naturally. Everyone could see the progression. Delia didn't.

Anna (Mary Catherine) was about fifteen months when it happened. After church one Sunday, Andy drove them home as usual. He parked in front of her house and turned the motor off. Anna had fallen asleep. He sat for a moment and didn't get out to get the door and baby as he usually would.

"What's the matter?" asked Delia. "Is everything okay?"

Andy didn't look at her and simply said, "No."

He didn't sound angry, nor did he look angry. He didn't look at her at all. His face was almost expressionless. They were both silent. Delia didn't want to ask, but ventured, "Well, something must be wrong. Why are we sitting here?"

"I want to ask you a question."

"Okay?" Her voice had a raised inflection showing her concern.

"Delia, you're a smart and capable woman, and of course, beautiful. Let's go out to dinner tonight, a nice dinner."

She wanted to laugh but didn't, sensing that would be the wrong reaction. His face was serious and in no way did she want to be hurtful. She was silent.

"What's the matter? I know I made a promise to give you space, no pressure, but that was almost two years ago now, even before Anna was born. You know how I feel. I think you've known that for a long time."

"Yes."

Andy pleadingly went on, "Yes, to which question?"

Delia simply smiled and answered, "Both."

So, it began. She knew things were different. Delia said yes to dinner but also yes to knowing how Andy felt.

There is nothing like your first love, nothing. Some are lucky enough to walk through life with that person, but not everyone gets that path. Love can find you. It may be different, but different can be good too, maybe minus the magic of firsts. Joy comes in many forms and flavors. Andy brought joy and meaning to Delia. To say she was grateful would never be enough.

Day 19

Alina hadn't experienced snow before, at least not like this. It wasn't even winter yet. It had started when she was at work; that made her nervous. Jax was alone. Snow would be new to him, too. She phoned the Johnsons and asked if they could get Jax out and feed him. Local weather stations posted travel advisories, and she didn't know when she would get home. Part of it depended on if everyone on the next shift could make it in. She mentioned she had never driven in the snow. Mrs. Johnson said to take it easy. The plows were good in town and that part of her trip should be fine.

There were about 6 inches at this point. That was a lot of snow to Alina, but laughable to everyone else when she heard the stories of the snowbanks in the storm of '66 or '72. It was almost incomprehensible. Gabe saw her looking out a window and assured her it would be fine. If she felt uneasy driving, he would get her home. That covered all the bases.

"Why don't we head down to the cafeteria and catch something to eat before it closes? Chances are we may be here for a while if the next shift is short help."

"Okay, I suppose you're right." How ridiculous she was to be nervous about it. No one around her was upset, maybe annoyed, but not really upset. As they headed down to the cafeteria and walked in, there were a few who had the same idea. The cafeteria wasn't as bad as the jokes about it. There was soup, salad, sandwiches, and decent cookies available for dessert. This was an excellent diversion.

A few minutes with Gabe, and she relaxed. Dinner was decent, and the company made up for anything else. As they headed upstairs, they were both paged. A serious car accident occurred, and the ER waited for several individuals who were coming in. There were three, two adults and one child, maybe around 8 years old. They headed upstairs and could hear the ambulances. Everything was in motion as the EMTs brought in the people. The woman was bleeding, a head injury. The child was unconscious and the man in the ambulance was stable, scratched up, and wincing in pain. He had gotten jostled around and maybe a few ribs were broken. Alina worked on the woman, who was very distressed, asking about her son. She needed stitches. There was no comforting her, so it was very hard to stitch her up. Finally, Alina put her hands on her shoulders and looked straight into the woman's eyes.

"Dr. Stewart is taking care of your son. I need to take care of you so you can be with him. Dr. Stewart is a fine doctor. He will help him. What's your son's name?"

The conversation seemed to calm the woman. Even though it stopped Alina from dealing with her wounds, the woman needed to calm down.

"Thomas, Tom."

"Good. Tom is in expert hands. Do you remember what happened?"

"The roads were terrible. We went into a skid. The car coming in the other direction, the headlights. I couldn't see or control it; we hit each other, and I spun off the road."

"It was an accident."

"Dr. Levin."

She turned, and it was Gabe.

"Hello, Mrs. Woods. Tom will be fine. The accident knocked him around somewhat. The impact when you hit the guardrails and the compression of the belt caused some injuries; when he hit his head, he passed out. He will be okay. That's the most important thing right now."

"Thank God. I'm so sorry. So sorry."

"That's only meant as information to help. The man in the other vehicle is fine, too. Some bruises. It was an accident. Please try to relax and let Dr. Levin stitch you up. She'll give you something for the pain. We need time now for everything to settle. Okay?"

The woman relaxed, and Alina made eye contact with Gabe. What she was giving for the pain would also act as a mild sedative. The accident could've been worse. Within the hour, the ER was quiet again. She saw the repercussions of bad weather in this early storm. Then, the lights flickered momentarily, a blackout followed. It took a few seconds for the generators to kick in.

Gabe looked at Alina and said, "Welcome to winter!"

She rolled her eyes, remembering. It was barely Thanksgiving. They were hopeful the power would return. For the moment, everyone was safe, and they were operable. Coffee sounded like a good next step. Hard to believe, but almost 3 hours had passed since dinner. Taking care of the accident victims, writing reports, and doing a quick check of the floors took up that time. A couple of people from the next shift had made it to work. By that time, others had called in. The news said that roads were becoming impassable. They had closed a few. With nightfall, storms become even more treacherous. The wind picked up, which put it at another level. It looked as if they would be at the hospital for the duration. A double shift, again.

Winter! Alina could understand why the staff was underwhelmed when she brought up snow. She knew there was a fun side. There had to be a fun side, or why else would people live here? She shook her head slightly. Time to move on. The accident caused commotion for a while and now that had passed. She was grateful.

The coming week brought the Christmas season and the town's tree lighting. Gabe had asked her to go. They were moving from awkward firsts to comfortable. A few months back, she would have run from this; she had plans. That's why she moved across the country. Her medical career came first, and there was the sideline, her family. Gabe was not uptight about either. He was one of the most relaxed people she knew and was easy, a friend first, one who was most needed in this new adventure and countryside. The week served as a further introduction to snow. The storm had left about 20-plus inches, and Alina had to learn about driving, parking, and even walking. That may sound strange, but where she was from in Texas, she saw nothing like it, but understood now where the fascination could wear off.

Entering the hospital, she felt ready. Because of the storm, the schedule shuffled. Everyone who worked the double shift had a day off, and she felt refreshed. The hospital seemed peaceful. The nurses agreed. They were relieved, too.

Alina would do her rounds. There were no new events or notes of concern. She saw the accident victims first. The mother and child were doing fine. Both were much calmer. A day's rest made a significant difference. The embarrassed woman regretted how she acted. Alina assured her it was understandable and not a problem. The boy was eager to go home; they had already discharged the man in the other vehicle. Unfortunately, the Covid patients were about the same.

Delia was the last to check and Alina was thinking about how she'd been there the longest. Turning into her room, she surprised the young doctor and was sitting in the chair by the window. She'd had her breakfast there. The woman stared blankly at her.

"How are you doing, Delia?"

"Fine."

"It's good to see you sitting up. This has been a hard spell for you."

"It has."

The woman stared without expression.

"Are you all right?"

"Don't worry, Doctor. I know who you are."

This took Alina by surprise. It must have shown on her face.

"I know you're not Anna. I've been in and out of it more than you know over the last couple of weeks."

Alina said she felt she had startled her at one point, and it appeared she reminded her of someone, Anna. She had hoped to talk with Karen, but the week got away from her with shift changes and the weather. The restrictions also made it difficult to talk with people who weren't coming for visits.

"I hope everything is well with your family. I know these are trying times."

Delia looked at her. Her look was intense, but soft at the same time. She wasn't angry or disturbed, more resolute.

"Anna was my daughter from my first marriage. Her father died in Vietnam. He never saw her. I was only eighteen years old. She was a wonderful baby."

"I'm sorry for your loss. I know there are some things we never get over. You learn to live with them and walk through the sorrow."

The old woman turned and looked more squarely at Alina. It was unnerving.

"You sound as if you know about sorrow."

"My mother passed away in Afghanistan. She was an army nurse."

Delia's expression changed.

"I'm not sure what happened to my daughter. We had a falling out. She was in the service."

"Family is complex," was the young doctor's response. She didn't know what else to say. For whatever reason, this woman was intermittently repelled to an earlier time, and it had affected her greatly. It was as if she was reliving it. Sickness can complicate things. Delia was in her late sixties, older but not elderly, as some might think. Today, she was sharp and clear on every detail. Any lack of expression was not a sign of cognitive loss. This was hard, but good. Her family was loving and concerned. They were waiting for this clarity to come. Though she wasn't strong, Alina was feeling more confident that the Covid crisis had passed for her. Being in bed for so long, Delia would need to get stronger, and home would be better than rehab. Contagion and reinfection were concerns. Getting home would be the best route if she were able. Alina believed she was, but past events and mild depression were affecting her.

"I've finished my first rounds. How would you like to go to the solarium? It's at the end of the hall. The sun's out and there are so many plants, it feels as if you're in a garden. What about it?"

This threw Delia, but Alina saw an ever so slight interest rise, and the weight of sadness drop. A lighter air came over her.

The trips down the hall to the solarium became physical and emotional therapy, happening multiple times a day. When Alina had time, she would accompany Delia, even if only for a little while. It was a beautiful area and could easily accommodate a few masked patients who needed some therapy. It was noticeable her demeanor was brighter. The pandemic saw an increase in extreme visitor restrictions. An obvious change came when patients could see family. It was almost a common occurrence; her daughter or son would come with the kids and stand outside the windows of the solarium. Even when it was not good weather, they came. The family restored her mood. Other families did the same. Isolation was one of the worst effects of the pandemic. People grabbed moments.

Alina enjoyed getting to know Delia and felt relieved at the prospect of her discharge. Many intubated or older patients didn't get to go home. The pandemic was raging. After the summer of the first year, people were more casual, less careful. Maneuvering the school year and its complications added more concern for spread.

Entering her room, Alina said, "Delia, how are you today?"

"Doing well, Doctor. I've enjoyed going out to the solarium and think it's helped me get back to my old self."

"I agree. You look brighter. Have you walked at all?"

"A little. Not as steady as I'd like. I feel I've made progress and hope to see more improvement soon."

"It doesn't have to be perfect. If you have some help at home, you should be fine. You'll also need to use a walker for a week or so."

"I'll stay with Karen for a few days while they're working on the farm. They're planning on setting up the main floor, so I don't have to do any stairs. Karen's son will come over. He's thirteen. If I'm going home to one floor and have company, by the time another week passes, I should almost be back to normal."

"Sounds like a plan. How about a walk around the solarium? Want to try?"

"Sure! Let's do it."

Alina bent over and told Delia to lean on her and they would stand for a minute before walking. An aide was passing and stopped in to say she could help. The walker was nearby, and extra hands were a good idea too. Alina leaned a little and reached under Delia's arms. A strange look came over her face. The young doctor couldn't decide what it meant. Fear? Pain? Whatever joy they had at the beginning was gone. She looked at the aide and signaled to get Delia back into her chair.

"What's the matter? What happened? Are you in pain?"

"Your locket? Where did you get it? How?"

It stunned Alina how distressed Delia had become. How could that happen? Why did it happen? Early on, she seemed to relate to Alina, calling her Anna. It all passed, and she continued to improve, so it wasn't anything that she discussed specifically with Karen, her daughter. But this...

A few of the older patients who were very sick would have emotional, almost delusional events. With high temperatures, and their isolation from family, it was a common occurrence. This was different. It was as if she catapulted back and lost all the ground over a locket.

Alina was the focus of the incident. The aide helped Delia back into the chair and settled her. Cami, the charge nurse, stopped in and could see something was up. She assisted Delia, but didn't miss the shock and distress of the doctor. Alina had stepped into the corridor. She just stood against the wall stiffly.

"What happened?"

"I don't know, Cami. Her progress impressed me. Socialization and movement everything was on track, more than on track. It was great to see her."

"Something happened. I caused it. I bent over to help her stand. When I did, my locket fell outside my shirt. That was the trigger."

Alina held the locket, which was unremarkable. Inside was a picture of her mother. The nurse's eyes widened; she stared at the picture and then at Alina.

"Is there any chance, did you show, or did Delia see the picture?"

"I don't remember it opening. It all happened so fast. I don't remember it opening."

The repetition and her face showed the young doctor's anxiety.

"What?"

"The eyes. The eyes look familiar."

"Familiar?"

"Can't you see?" Cami saw her confusion.

"See what?"

She pointed it out. Alina's mother and Delia. The picture was of her mother in Afghanistan. The smile, her eyes. It could have triggered something.

"But she didn't see it. She didn't see the picture."

Cami looked and quietly said, "She saw you. Many times. Something similar happened with you, but she was very sick then. Things like this occur with people who have been seriously ill, right? "

Alina went back into Delia's room. She was quiet. The aide looked and, with her eyes expressed, she didn't know what was going on. Alina carefully approached. Delia turned.

"I'm okay. I won't fall apart."

This startled the young woman, but she remained calm and waited.

"You remind me of someone, my daughter. When I look at you, there have been times I see her and it's startling, like seeing a ghost."

"I'm sorry."

Alina couldn't think of anything else to say.

"I would never want to upset you. You're almost ready to go home. I wasn't aware..."

"Of course, you weren't trying to do anything. Why would you? I'll be fine. I just need to go home. How long has it been?"

"Three weeks tomorrow, exactly. I needed to do a checkup today. You are lucid and recognize your surroundings. Looking at your chart, blood pressure and vitals have been good. Eyeing that lunch tray, you could eat better."

Delia almost smiled, saying the food was lacking, and she would be fine when she got home. Alina acknowledged they had her on a simple diet after coming out of the virus and being intubated. Overall, there was progress.

"Let me look at the rest of your blood work and reports. You have to stand and walk, with help at least to start. It would be understandable to need help. I know we were about to try that when we ran into our misunderstanding."

"Misunderstanding?"

Seeing her knowing expression, Alina responded, "Okay, I'll be back later. Honestly, it wouldn't be today, but we'll look at later tomorrow or the next day for your discharge."

The hope of going home satisfied Delia. Hope is a powerful motivator. For the moment, Alina felt she could move forward. Peace returned, and it settled everything. She had a reason to call Karen, Delia's daughter. It wasn't about someone coming out of an illness. The physical assessment was suitably strong, but the emotional side left questions. She would call at the end of her shift.

The rest of the day couldn't pass fast enough. Alina sensed an uneasy feeling. Gabe was on his way out and wondered what she was doing. She explained she would finish up some things and would be maybe an hour before getting out. He asked if she wanted to catch dinner; the look on her face was uncertain. Gabe knew when to let things go. He said, "Okay," and offered that she could call later if she felt like it.

Alina dialed Karen's number, and it went to voicemail. *That was typical.* When you want to deal with something, roadblocks! She left a brief message about wanting to discuss Delia's discharge and that she would try again, or Karen could call. Ironically, as she walked out of the office and turned, Karen was heading down the hallway.

"I just left a message for you."

Karen looked concerned and asked if everything was all right with her mother.

"Yes, I didn't mean to worry you, but I wondered if you had a few minutes. I'd like to discuss something."

Karen was willing and very grateful she could come in. Today the hospital started permitting one visitor per patient, masked, and they limited the time.

Alina invited her into the office. She quickly assured her the physical progress and vitals were good, which is why they were looking at a discharge. Karen's eyes seemed to wait for the but or whatever was coming.

Alina said, "I think I upset her today, and it wasn't the first time."

Now Karen was leaning in and said,

"I don't understand."

"When we intubated Delia, she drifted in and out of consciousness; that's not uncommon. I would check on her, and we would make eye contact. Suddenly she would become distressed, restless. It seemed as if something was on her mind. She would reach for my arm. Patients are fearful in the hospital and that's typical. Under current circumstances, the masks, and isolation, made it worse, but this was with me. I asked the other staff to watch for it and it only happened with me. It didn't happen every time and her overall health improved. We've been going down to the solarium. You, Tim, and your children were at those windows, and she enjoyed it, and I believe it helped her healing process. The last thing I wanted to work on was her walking. I explained I would help her stand and we could go for a short walk. She was up for it."

Karen listened intently, not having any idea where the doctor was heading. Alina explained she asked Delia to stand and that she would steady her with her arms under Delia's.

"We started this, and she looked squarely at me with such sorrow, saying, 'Anna'? Any strength she had evaporated instantly. Within minutes, it was as if nothing had happened. Delia was totally lucid and knew who I was. Any thoughts about why this reaction? Everything else seems on track except for these moments."

Karen didn't speak right away. She noted she wasn't sure what to say. "I had an older sister. Delia was married when she was seventeen and became pregnant. Her husband was drafted and sent to Vietnam. He was killed shortly after he arrived there. The baby was a girl. She named her Mary Catherine, but I remember when she was angry, her parent voice would say 'Anna'. That was her middle name. No wait, Annaliese. My sister was insistent, though, on being called Mary Kate."

Alina didn't respond. She stood frozen. Her hand felt for the locket and unlatched it. Karen was confused and asked if she was all right.

"Dr. Levin. Dr. Levin..."

Alina opened the locket. Slowly but without hesitancy she asked, "Is this your sister?"

Karen looked and didn't need to say anything.

Day 20

Alina finished the shift and wanted to leave. It was too much to process. She felt as if she was in a movie. Cami and others could see something was wrong but kept a distance. All she wanted was to get out of the building, even dreading the thought she might run into Gabe. Alina knew she would have to confront everything, but not now. It was later fall and nights were colder than she was used to, but her only thought was to get Jax and go for a walk. Shedding her work clothes, making coffee, and breaking out some chocolate was a good transition. She headed out to the park, not even thinking about the snow that still covered the ground. Other than a few diehards, it was mostly empty and belonged to her. Right now, she needed that.

When she saw Karen's reaction to the locket, everything became clear. Alina's mom was Karen's older sister and Delia's first child with her beloved Mike. The exchange was brief. She knew she would have to talk to Karen and Delia. She had cut the conversation short, even before discussing Delia's discharge with any detail. This was not what she expected. It was always in the back of her mind. Her mother had been from this area and the thought was someday... that came sooner and unexpectedly. Why should she be surprised? The mountains were an expansive region, but the population was not dense.

199

She's a doctor and in the middle of a pandemic, with hospitals and clinics available in a very limited way. She had always been curious but never considered it plausible or likely that she would run into family, not like this. Now what?

After about an hour of head-clearing, she headed home. Cooking was a go to stress reliever, and she started the fixings for soup, a quick version. Her grandmother had taught her a lot about cooking shortcuts. There was a knock at the door, which she could have expected. Alina opened it, paused for a moment, and smiled, waving Gabe in.

"Thought you could use some dinner."

"Have soup cooking but it will be a while, so, yes; dinner sounds good."

The dinner was simple: antipasto and pizza. When stressed and after a brisk walk, that was gladly accepted rather than waiting for soup. She would save the broth. Conversation was light. Gabe was treading carefully, not having many details of what had occurred, only what the nurses observed.

"Wanna talk?"

"No! Yes," Alina replied, looking distressed, but knowing eventually she would have to deal with this. It might as well be with Gabe.

"I didn't really expect anything to happen. It was in my head... finding my relatives sometime, maybe, but never right now. Delia's reactions make sense. She saw my mother when she looked at me. When she was between worlds, conscious but not, it was delusional but had threads of reality."

"It happens when people are out of it."

"I know."

"So, what now?"

"I don't know."

Alina struggled with that. She had left Karen standing there. Gabe gently told her that the nurses paged him, and he finished the discussion about Delia's discharge. Unless something physically changes, she could go home tomorrow. They were looking at later in the day, which would give Alina time for any input she may have. He agreed that physically Delia was fairly strong. Confusion, after all she had been through, would not be uncommon, and home with familiar surroundings could be very helpful. The discharge was the straightforward part. Now the question was what to do with the rest, the family part.

"Just talk. Meet with Karen first. You have no idea of the history behind the family. Be a listener. I'm sure they will have questions for you. That would be the starting point."

Of course, Gabe was right. It sounded simple, but he knew it wouldn't be. There was an estrangement. Wounds that never healed would surface. That was easy to figure when you consider Delia's distress at seeing Alina. Nor would it be simple for her to accept she was the trigger for the old woman's grief. Forget old woman; it was her grandmother's grief. What about her mother? What got them to the point of a complete break? Karen would be the best place to start. Alina would call in the morning. They would need a plan to bring Delia up to date. Steps. How do you bridge the years and distance? A concern for Alina was what effect this would have on Delia's progress. It was undeniable that there had been a connection from the beginning. Alina had never dreamed what that would be. She thought Delia was a fighter; that her family cared... and she, as a doctor in a small community hospital, was getting the experience she hoped for—more time with her patients. This changed things. Memories were playing a part in the old woman's stability. Alina could turn apparent progress into a trauma inducing event. Steps. But the question was, how to begin?

Delia answered that question readily. She wanted out of the hospital as soon as possible. She didn't appear angry or concerned and even joked with some of the staff, telling Cami she could finally get rid of her and free up some time. It appeared she was emotionally ready, but that's before Alina, as her doctor, prepared the discharge papers and had the final check. Alina was nervous and couldn't think about what to say.

Possibly, the best way to start was to do the expected exam; sign off on the discharge and take cues from there. She headed down the hall.

The door was ajar. She knocked gently and entered. It was early afternoon, and the remains of lunch were on the tray. Delia smiled peacefully.

"Good afternoon. How are you feeling today?"

"Feeling pretty good, but will be better when I get home. I know I have a road ahead, but my kids have set up the lower floor of my house. I won't go there first. The plan is to spend a few days with Karen. They are working out the rest."

"We can set up physical therapy for you. Someone will come to Karen's and help you with exercises that will show you how to get stronger. Your vitals are good; you have a plan for going home safely. I think that covers the most important things. Having a good family support system is at the top of the list and you have that. I feel comfortable discharging you, but want you to come back for a follow-up here or with your primary in a week. It's important that happens. We'll send all the information home in your papers. We are aiming for later this afternoon. Dr. Stewart said that Karen had some last minute details to take care of at home. I will make sure everything is ready. That's about it."

"I don't think so," said Delia, looking squarely at Alina, who had no other words. Her heart pounded, but she gave no reaction. Everything was surreal. The surroundings faded against the face of the old woman. No sign of fear or disorientation presented. Delia was resolute. Strength was the formidable message.

"I'm quite in my right mind, if you're wondering. I know who you are; there's no question, though you might have a few."

Alina thought and said, "I have a few. But first, I never wanted to upset you. It wasn't until..."

Cutting in, Delia said, "I know; until I fell apart, you couldn't have had any idea. I like to think maybe this was providence."

"Providence?"

"Yes, I'm not big on coincidence. There was more here than we both could have expected. I have long regretted decisions I made regarding your mother. Those early days were so difficult. I loved her father and so much happened to us in such a short time. I got through those days only by the grace of God. They were the most traumatic in my life. I wasn't even seventeen when I met your grandfather, not much more than a child."

Alina stood there listening, not knowing what to say or do. She wasn't a part of that time, so couldn't have changed anything. But now, Delia could see the distress in her face, her granddaughter's face. She tapped the bed, encouraging Alina to sit. After the slightest pause, she did not consider how this might look to a passerby.

"It was the locket. I didn't even have to look at the picture, just seeing the locket and your eyes. That was enough. I gave it to her for her eighteenth birthday. Tell me about your mother."

That was the question Alina dreaded.

"My mother passed away when I was twelve. She was an army nurse, a lieutenant in Afghanistan. She was an exceptional nurse and mom. My father's parents, the Levins, raised me; my father is still in the service. I lived in the south for most of my life, Texas. After medical school, I wanted a change; all I knew was that my mother came from the Adirondacks in New York. I also wanted a smaller hospital so I could have time to get to know my patients more, and a position opened here."

Delia looked down while Alina was speaking. That was worrisome, but she proved there was no need for concern.

"The last time we spoke, she wanted to enlist, and I couldn't even consider it. The only thing I remember was how much our family had already sacrificed. I wouldn't listen. I set up a wall. It wasn't for discussion. I gave her the silent treatment. It was an uneasy peace in the house, avoiding the topic. When she graduated from high school, she left home. Her strategy was to get her nursing degree in the service and see what opportunities came her way. She tried to keep in touch. I wouldn't budge and closed her out. How I have regretted that! When she left, that was it. I was so angry, not even so much at her, but the whole military thing. Her letters stopped. I didn't know she went overseas or that she married, and her name changed. It wasn't like today. There was no Internet or cell phones. Finding people wasn't as easy. I kept thinking somehow everything would work out. Time passed. I'm sorry; if I could change it, I would. I'm sorry for your loss."

Alina could see Delia's deep regret. She could hear it in her voice. There were no answers for the past, only what this history would hold for their future. There was silence.

"I don't know what to say," was all that Alina could get out. How do you deal with intense emotions when you are like an outsider looking in? Her mother was the connecting factor, but until now, neither knew the other existed.

All that she could offer is why don't we focus on getting you home first? Delia nodded and agreed. She grabbed Alina's hand. "You'll come and visit?" The response was a smile and the old woman relaxed. So much to think about. Alina put the paperwork together and signed off on Delia's discharge. Karen would pick her up in the afternoon.

The rest of the day was uneventful. Alina was glad. Karen was on time. Tim was out in the parking lot with two of the grandkids. It was satisfying to have a victory, to see someone go home. One patient had changed Alina's life forever. Her expectations were just that, expectations but not assurances. They were a sideline hoping to lead to a new life and job. The Adirondacks were a rural but expansive area, and finding a family with almost no direct leads seemed impossible. But then again, nothing is impossible when faith is involved. Apparently, that's what both her grandmothers believed.

It wasn't closure as she had imagined. There were no simple words to express how she felt, only an uncertainty that wasn't negative or distressing, just unknown.

Day 21

3 weeks! How is it possible for so much to have happened? Alina had no regrets. Events and decisions were what they were. Though some were overwhelming, others were in line with the life and career she hoped to secure with her move to the mountains. And, of course, there were surprises. Delia was a surprise. They followed through with the discharge. It had only been a couple of days, but she had checked in with Karen and all was going well. Delia was slow but making progress and was determined to gain back her strength. Alina had expected nothing less. The family invited her for dinner. She couldn't get over feeling awkward, but it was for the upcoming weekend. There were still a few days to process what potential outcomes could be. How do you walk into the home of people who are family, but you just met? Alina couldn't quite get her head around it. Thank God for work! Literally.

The hospital remained busy from Covid and the regular problems. Seasonal allergies, accidents, and school related illnesses hadn't decreased. She got a taste of what winter might bring. For now, it was still fall and beautiful except for the surprise snowstorm.

Late morning brought a text from Karen. They would have dinner at the farm, out of town. She sent the directions and time. This caught Alina off guard since she wondered about Delia being back home but knew Karen must have a plan. She noted the change, and the day went on, but was wondering what to bring. A contribution gave another focus and eased anxiety. Not knowing much about the family, ice cream seemed a reasonable choice. Who doesn't like ice cream? There would be several kids between Karen and Tim, so it was easy! That settled it. Ice cream!

The week passed. They all seem to, with no shortage of events or activities. It was amazing how very rural the area was. Within minutes, the town disappeared, and the mountains towered. The scenery provided pastoral and mountainous views that were outstanding. She easily found the turn, which led to a small, rough secondary road. There were few houses, but she knew she was heading to the end of the road for the farm. As Alina rounded the bend, a beautiful picture appeared. From a distance, she could see Delia on the porch and children playing in the front yard. The surrounding land went on forever. The buildings were neat and pristinely kept. When she pulled off to the side to park, she saw Delia, smiling.

"Well, I didn't expect to see you here. It looks as if farm life agrees with you."

Delia perked up. "We've made some changes. Tim is moving here, so I will stay on the farm."

Alina's face lit up, "What a perfect situation! Obviously, the kids love it. I can see that you do as well."

"I'm quite content and have always loved it here. Such peace! I looked for a way to find that and settle my past. Some things we can control; others we can't. This will keep the homestead going. I've always seen it as a gathering place."

Alina had a sense of calm. Delia wanted her to sit, but she noted the ice cream saying she would run it in first. As she grabbed for the door, it opened before her. It was Gabe, in an apron and carrying a plate of meat.

Alina was more than surprised. "What are you doing here?"

He gave the sensible answer, "Grilling! I helped Tim with moving some things, so I got invited. You know what a skilled cook I am. It stands to reason."

Alina glanced over at Delia, who was smiling. Perhaps this road wouldn't be as uncertain or different as she thought. In so many ways, it had been a stormy few weeks. Dark and formidable. Maybe Delia was right in saying she didn't believe in coincidences, but in Providence. Things may be different, but she was home... so was Alina.

The Silent Storm

Eases in like a wave
catching our senses
while building strength.
Applying pressure
that immobilizes.
Details lost in the fray
create spaces
while building and breaking
a different road,
still leading home.

www.ingramcontent.com/pod-product-compliance
Lightning Source LLC
Chambersburg PA
CBHW060433180626
46817CB00007B/2800